the goat
in the tree

ESSENTIAL PROSE SERIES 103

Guernica Editions Inc. acknowledges the support of the Canada Council
for the Arts and the Ontario Arts Council. The Ontario Arts Council
is an agency of the Government of Ontario.

We acknowledge the financial support of the Government of Canada
through the Canada Book Fund (CBF) for our publishing activities.

the goat in the tree

LORNE ELLIOTT

GUERNICA
TORONTO • BUFFALO • LANCASTER (U.K.)
2014

Michael Mirolla, editor
David Moratto, interior book designer
Guernica Editions Inc.
P.O. Box 76080, Abbey Market, Oakville, (ON), Canada L6M 3H5
2250 Military Road, Tonawanda, N.Y. 14150-6000 U.S.A.

Distributors:
University of Toronto Press Distribution,
5201 Dufferin Street, Toronto (ON), Canada M3H 5T8
Gazelle Book Services, White Cross Mills, High Town, Lancaster LA1 4XS U.K.

First edition.
Printed in Canada.

Legal Deposit – First Quarter
Library of Congress Catalog Card Number: 2013947109

Library and Archives Canada Cataloguing in Publication

Elliott, Lorne, author
The goat in the tree / Lorne Elliott.

(Essential prose series 103)
Issued in print and electronic formats.
ISBN 978-1-55071-810-2

I. Title. II. Series: Essential prose series ; 103

PS8609.L5495G63 2014   C813'.6   C2013-905503-7   C2013-905504-5

DIDN'T REALIZE I was hungry till I smelled cooking from across the street. Through the open gate of the ryad I could see a table crowded with brochettes of mutton and baskets of sliced bread. There were also plates of black olives, sliced tomatoes, honey-soaked phylo pastry for dessert and glasses of white wine to wash everything down. It was as good a place as any to get back into the game.

Inside the courtyard, guests in formal wear stood around a fountain in small groups, but between them and me two men in tuxedos stood outside the gate, one smoking a cigarette, one with his foot on the raised threshold of the door. The gatekeepers.

"Max," I introduced myself. "Sorry I'm late. I was just across town buying a silk scarf for my daughter." There was no scarf, I didn't have a daughter, and my name isn't Max.

"That's fine," said the one with the cigarette.

"So. Where is she?

"Portia?"

"Who else?" And then to soften that I added: "I must look like a bum." And smiled.

"Not at all," he said, which was promising.

"I was painting," I explained, though I didn't know what this meant yet. I've always found the best way to fill your head with ideas is to surprise yourself.

"What medium are you using?" said his friend.

"Seashells," I said without hesitation.

"Ah! That blue."

"Yes. A bit of a cliché now, of course, but the tourists seem to like it." As long as I remember I could always do this. Accept what they said, see the world they presented, and add to it like I was from that world too.

The other man was less interested in art, and he had looked away. "There's Portia there," he said. So I nodded a see-you-later and stepped over the threshold into the courtyard. It was like stepping from one country into another. Outside was Morocco, this was France.

Beside the food table a lady of a certain age stood like a hawk in a tree, surveying her party, temporarily alone.

"Portia!" I said, all breezy familiarity.

Her face turned, beaming a sudden neutral smile. She didn't have a clue who I was (how could she?) and I saw a moment of panic when she thought that she *should* know me. "Oh," she said. "It's you! Hello!" And I was in.

"I wish I'd brought something," I said, "but since Dahlia went away ..." And I left it hanging, then snapped out of it. "Anyhow, nice ryad you have here. Absolutely prime."

"Thank you, and don't worry. Nobody brought gifts. It's not that type of party. How *is* Dahlia?"

I thought of an interesting way to start the story: "Well, I haven't heard, of course ..." But she didn't want to hear any more.

"No, of course not. And you probably haven't been eating properly, am I right?"

"Thank you, Portia. I *am* a tad peckish."

"Right over there. Don't be shy." So although my story had failed, my desired ends were achieved.

Whoever braised those brochettes really knew what they were doing. It was the marinade. Wine, herbes de Provence, cumin. I was tempted, but it wouldn't do to just plunge in and stuff them all back at once. What was needed was the delicate touch. Nibble the meat off the first skewer. Heaven. A quick glance around, wolf the rest and get another brochette into my paw. Nibble nibble. Now a cough. Look around as though for something to wet the throat. What's this? Wine. Just what was called for.

Taste first, don't swill. A bit young, but the real thing. Vouvray. And with that first taste, I remembered the train out from Gare d'Austerlitz to Amboise, a trip with a friend of my father to fish for gardon just north of there. I remembered the soil the colour of old ivory, and the flint in the fords that hurt your bare feet when you waded across, the maisons troglodytes on the limestone escarpments, the hot uplands, the poplar in the valleys. Independent of everything else going on in my head, a setting for a story started to gather.

A man appeared at my side. "Well, this is nice," he said, not looking at me.

"Yes. Portia does it up in style, doesn't she?"

"She certainly does."

"How did *you* meet her?" I asked, which presupposed that I was legitimate.

"Nephew. You?"

"She's a fan."

"Performer?"

"All the world is a stage, of course, but no. Artist. Seashells." The wine and food were working. Creativity flourished. "Excellent food, incidentally. These brochettes? Goat?"

"Mutton," he corrected, which I knew already, but he was watching me eat closely, studying, and what harm would it do if I gave him the opportunity to air this knowledge? "I wish I wasn't dieting," he said, which explained the look he was giving the food. Maybe a drinking problem he was fighting, too. "Try the salad," he added, to enjoy it vicariously.

"I'd better polish this off first," I said. "I wouldn't want to follow the salad with the wine." And I downed what remained in the glass. As a favour to him, you understand.

"All these rules," he said. "For instance, why *not* white wine with meat? Where did that prejudice come from, anyway?"

I said: "Louis the 14th always had white wine with his." Which may well have been true for all I knew.

"Assuming he knew anything about food," he said.

"Quite. He certainly had access to a lot, and a lot of different kinds, but that doesn't necessarily make you an expert. *'A full larder will only confuse the ... decision making'.*" But I had broken the rhythm, scrambled for a word. "It's better in the original," I covered, as though I'd been translating. He smiled and I think was about to ask from what language, but I cut him off. "Max." I introduced myself.

"I know."

So he'd been talking with people. It was even possible that he'd been sent over to find out more about me. I wiped my fingers on a napkin and held out my hand: "I don't think I've had the pleasure."

"Lars," he said. No last name either, until he got mine. The wealthy. Their guard is up all the time. And why not? There are a lot of con men out there.

"The point is," I continued, "it's like they told us in high school, all about the ability to make choices. Take my cousin: four degrees from four different universities. Very book-smart."

"Couldn't make his mind up?" he asked and I felt a nibble on the line.

"Not for the longest time. Then, when he was fifty years old, he dropped it all and took up welding."

"What? Sculpture?"

"No, that's the thing. Shop work. Nine to five, five days a week. And Fridays he goes to the Café de La Gare, takes a table outside with his mates, drinks beer and sings off-key. He's happy." A heart-warming tale. Nostalgia for the mud. When the top floors are taken, check out the service rooms.

A gleam glowed in his eye and the plank that kept his shoulders rigid relaxed. He raised his eyebrows in an accepting flash. Happiness, the only currency. Then it was his turn to offer something, but nothing was there, and in that moment of panic I saw the family resemblance to Portia.

"A friend of mine from Aquitaine," I suggested. "He went to live with the gypsies. His family were *very* pleased."

"Tolstoy's brother," he said, for his pump had just needed some priming. He was one of those people who needed a springboard into a story, either another book, film, or play, to get his imagination up and running. A vicarious life. But he had a good audience in me. I had to draw him out. The salad really was excellent. Day old tomatoes in olive oil. A sprinkle of parsley. I had not run into this dressing before either. Olive oil, and ... fennel, that was it. Numbed the edges of my tongue slightly. Light, fresh and enhancing.

So I listened intently. He started in academic mode, rocking on his toes, straightening his body into podium stance. "Gregor Tolstoy," he said. "Lived with a Gypsy girl in the slums of St Petersburg. There is a theory that all Tolstoy's religious writings, his feelings for the poor, were an attempt to at least attain a sympathy for the people his brother attained just by living like them."

"More to it than that, of course." As I know he knew, I implied. "But how interesting. Certainly one of the wellsprings which contributed to the flood."

"Yes. And you're right. It's never as simple as that."

He was a rich kid who had made himself an expert in something, and now he needed an audience for all the books he'd read and shows he'd weathered. But he had no vocation, poor bastard. (Remember, I told myself. Sympathy is everything. Contempt is death.) Besides, I liked him. And I liked him more as he talked on, came by way of Tolstoy's brother, through hints and allusions at first, and then more explicitly, to his own life. And finally, he was a friend. Well, you can't have too many of them.

But some humour was called for. "Then there's René Montjoie," I said, smiling.

"Who?"

"You never heard? The Marxist?"

"No."

"A while ago now ...," I said, which is one way of saying: 'Once upon a time'. "He was working with the Left. Became disenchanted with the politics, not left*ism*, you understand, but office politics. So he went directly to the workers. Hit the farms for the grape harvest. Solidarity with the field hands. Had all the goodwill in the world, but none of the skill. Bought himself a 2CV Camionnette, a heap of junk. The compression was so bad he had to push it up hills. No handle on the door, so when he grabbed the window frame to pull the door shut, the hinged window would fall closed, smacking his knuckles." I did a quick mime to illustrate while I said it, and was rewarded with a laugh. Heads turned from other conversations around the courtyard, the sound of laughter starting to charge the magnet. "But he didn't let that stop him. Part of the experience. No problem. Friend of a cousin had a vineyard. He wanted to re-order society so that all people had access to all things, but he still had to use family ties to get to work in a vineyard. An imperfect world. He'd get that changed when the new dawn broke."

"So, why couldn't he?" said somebody who'd joined us. It was a foregone conclusion that he couldn't, my tone of voice suggested: Life is bigger than any individual's conception of it. But it was not to be a tragedy, not this story. The Mock Grandiose was what was called for here, setting up for a fall.

"It wasn't so much a 'cooperative' as it was an 'antagonistic'," I said. "There were the people who picked the grapes and there were the people who took the grapes to the presses. There were the people who pressed the wine and the people who drew the wine into vats, where the yeast started to work. Thanks to René, everybody that year saw where they were on the social ladder of the winemaking operation, and so of course wanted a higher rung. They started to grumble. Held meetings, elected a shop steward. Voted for a strike."

I was drawing a crowd, so I started to play bigger, casting the net wider. "They were putting it to the owners, and there was nothing the owners could do." Danger of politics now, so some fantasy was necessary. I dropped my voice, which had the effect of drawing those who were listening closer.

"The confrontation was at the bernache, the first tasting. With the work slowdowns and disruptions, it hadn't been a good year. What should have been a celebration was stressful and suspicious. Management were milling uneasily with the workers, and the priest who blessed the harvest was making no headway trying to reconcile anybody. René had his glass filled by the head vintner, raised it to his lips, took the first sip and ... took it away from his lips and looked at it. He was puzzled. He took another small sip. What was wrong? A murmur rose in the crowd. He handed his glass to the head vintner, who took a sip. 'No,' he said, and sipped again and frowned, then cast the rest of the wine in the glass onto the ground."

"Bad?" said Lars.

"It was still only grape juice," I said. "They called in a viticulturist, who tasted and discussed and advanced a theory. Next came an expert in oenology from the university who took from the back of his car a microscope, smeared some of the wine onto a glass plate and put it under the lens. He looked in, adjusted the focus, invited the priest who looked in and who started back, disbelieving. The Head Vintner was next with the same reaction, and then the owner, who just kept looking, amazed ..."

I paused, dead serious.

"What did they see?" said someone in my audience.

I looked up. "Thousands of yeast cells picketing." My audience relaxed and smiled. "One yeast-cell, at the head of the yeasts, addressed the crowd of yeasts in front of him. 'You eat the sugar and excrete alcohol, but what do *you* get out of it?' the head yeast cell demanded.

"And all the other yeast cells chanted: 'Nothing!'

"'And what are we going to do?'

"'Nothing!'

"'Louder!'

"'Nothing!'

"And under the great banner of 'Nothing' they went on strike. The yeast refused to eat the sugar, the grape juice never changed into alcohol and the wine was never made. And so the barrels were emptied, their contents thrown out on the fields where it fertilized for next year the beautiful vineyards of the Vouvray region."

Partly as a toast, I held my glass so it caught the sun, and downed the rest of the wine. Thank you. I couldn't have done it without you. And from the crowd that had gathered there was a smattering of applause.

They started to break up. Lars tapped his glass on mine. "Chin chin," he said.

"At least the yeast in this wine never went on strike," I said and saw that somebody else had come close: Portia, who was entranced.

"Where was that story from?" she asked.

"What story?" I said. "Gospel truth, every word."

"Did you create it?"

But it does no good to interrogate the Muse, so I had to dodge. "Assembled it," I said.

"Just now?"

"Well you know, the more you tell something, the better it gets." I found myself thinking that the wealthy always want to know how to get to the source, so they can own it. But what the hell do I really know about the wealthy? They were nice people here. They couldn't help what they were born into. And the food and drink were excellent. And free, or at least for the cost of a story.

I did have to shake her loose now though. "No," I said. "I heard it last time I was in France."

I dropped in status, but I had also slipped through her net. I was not as interesting as she had thought. Good.

We talked of other things. Our group broke up. I mingled. I told some other stories to other people.

I went over into the shade and leant against the wall to watch the shadows rise up the other side of the courtyard. I found myself beside an opening in the outer wall like a window, screened over with wood lattice through which I could hear on the street one of the caterers from the party, on a break, talking with a friend. "... Bus tour from Marrakech," I overheard his friend say.

"How are they?" said the caterer.

"They're a *bus* tour," said the first with a sigh.

And the caterer said: "Ah," understanding. "Who are you with now?"

"Mogador. Two more hours and we start back. You wouldn't like to take them, would you?"

"No. I have to be here tomorrow."

"You see, there's a gazelle ..." Meaning a girl.

Which was all very interesting. Food is one thing, but travel, in many ways, is more difficult. So I moved along my side of the wall and when I got to the gate I ducked out of the ryad, then took the first alley away from where the two friends were, into the souk. Once in, I took every left, walked along a dogleg street then left again, passed one alley further and found myself back on the main boulevard. I turned toward the gate again and almost bumped into the two friends, still standing there talking.

"Tour guide?" I asked.

"Yes. We'll be leaving in an hour," he said, thinking I was one of his customers.

"Not tonight," I said and then introduced myself. "I'm Eric Martin." He looked at me, waiting. "You're with Mogador Bus Tours, right?"

"Yes. Aziz," he introduced himself.

"Well, you won't be leaving tonight. Motor broke down."

"Motor?"

"That new double flange belt on the differential," I explained. "That bus isn't going anywhere."

"But … That's … too bad …" meaning that it was excellent. His friend smiled. "They're putting them up somewhere?" he said, feigning concern for his charges.

"Can't say. I'm sure they will. Where are they now?"

"It's their free hour. They'll be by the tourism board after five o'clock."

"Well, they're my worry now. You're off duty. You have a place for tonight?"

"Yes," he said, and he smiled again.

"Tomorrow at the tourist board, then. Say eleven?"

"I'll be there."

I probably should have gone back to the party and said goodbye to everybody, but I didn't want to push my luck. I started down the boulevard, past blue doors under the slanting sun. Shops on every corner, and in the alleys and side-streets craft stalls and bad plaster falling in patches off the walls. I walked toward the Place Moulay El Hassan, past those five great thuya trees. Outside the City Gates, a breeze from the ocean was blowing over the walls. Gulls over the port squeaked and squealed. I turned south, towards the Sqala du Port where the small blue boats are moored together, bobbing like blue seeds in an eddy. Essaouira. And now it was time to leave.

HE BUS WAS parked by a restaurant over-looking the beach, near where they build those big wooden boats. Around the bus there was a small crowd, and when I leant through the door I could see two or three passengers already seated.

"Sayeed?" I asked the driver. I had read his name-tag.

"Yes?"

"I'll be guiding them in this time. Aziz won't be making it."

"Really?"

"Yes. They phoned me from Marrakech. This *is* Mogador Tours, isn't it?" I leant back and looked at the side of the bus to check. He was about to ask some more questions, I think, or worse, phone in to check up on me, so I kept talking: "Aziz was supposed to meet a girl."

He nodded knowingly.

"He was waiting out on the street, and a donkey cart ran over his foot."

"No!"

"Yes. Broke it."

He looked concerned. "Is he all right?"

"Fine. Just his small toe. But the girl he was waiting for saw the whole thing."

"No!"

"Yes. He was cursing, limping around on the street. It somewhat damaged the romantic image he was trying to create. She had to take him to the hospital."

Now he laughed out loud. "Aziz!" he said. He could see it. Everything was all right.

"Anyhow," I said. "He phoned Mogador. Mogador phoned me. I'm taking Aziz's place. Charles." I held out my hand and he shook it.

I came on board and sat in the seat right behind him. I looked out the window at the sea and, as the departure time approached, the customers gathered and climbed on board in groups. First was a husband and wife, sixty years old, down from somewhere I wouldn't know until I heard them speak. Their children had all grown up now, the last one had just left for college. This was the first vacation alone since their honeymoon. They'd always wanted to come to Morocco.

Next came a woman who sat down and tried to figure out a digital camera, clicking a screen, tilting up her glasses, consulting a small manual, clicking again, putting it down in frustration, and leaning her back against the window and looking out, just remembering what she saw rather than trying to record it, as peace settled over her. A schoolteacher.

Then a man with a wife, a business woman who was making a list of figures in a small book, her expenses. A doctor, lawyer or accountant. Choose one, and once you've chosen, stick with it. This was all guesswork, of course, but more important than getting the facts was to build up a story around each, making them real, if only for myself. As they came on board and took their seats I was struck by the number of people in the world and the fewness of the types, though possibly that is not the human race's limitation, but mine.

Then I saw somebody striding angrily across the plaza toward us with a girl behind who was trying to get him to calm down. Trouble. She was dressed in clothes which tried not to be just presentable but sexy for him. He was dressed to do the same for her, but with less success. Both were dishevelled from their exertions. They weren't married. The girl was younger, and trying to make it work. The guy? Maybe he wasn't like this all the time, although it's no good saying that. You had to work with what you have.

I tried to think how this story would play itself out, the better to keep future events in control. I suppose that's how prophets work. I watched them approach and warned myself not to react to their anger.

He saw me through the window and strode towards the door, climbed onto the bus and addressed me directly.

"I would like to register a complaint," he said. "Are you who I talk to about that?"

There was something strange about his skin: It was orange. The result, perhaps, of having something go wrong when using instant tanning cream. It was distracting.

"I can certainly bring any issues you may have to the attention of the management of Mogador Tours," I said.

"You don't deal with them yourself?"

"Well, of course it depends ..."

"Covering your own ass, then," he said with a snort.

"What is the complaint exactly, sir?" It was important to use that "sir," and not sarcastically. I was only here to be of service.

"It's really all right ...," said the girl.

"No, it isn't," he said testily, dealing here with the important business of keeping the help in line. But I must not get in any sort of fight with him.

"Really," said the girl. "It was my bracelet."

"I can handle it."

She hadn't said he couldn't handle it. She said that it was all right. But he had ignored that, better to allow him to act like the implication had been insulting. *Once upon a time there was a man who was manipulative, temperamental, spoiled, and angry.* This had the makings of a decent Good-and-Evil story, but that view of things can hurt how you approach problems in the real world. Remember sympathy, I thought. *But he was all these things for a reason. When somebody is trying to humiliate somebody, it is always because they themselves have been humiliated.*

"Her bracelet was stolen," he said.

"Or I lost it," she said.

"Stolen. I've got this, Hélène."

She sighed and stood there, looking away, putting up with it.

"Did you witness the alleged theft?" I said, like I was taking the proper steps.

"It's not 'alleged'. I'm *telling* you."

"Did you witness the theft?" I said, graciously accepting his description of the event.

"No."

So it *was* alleged, then, wasn't it? but "Ah," was all I said, sympathy for her loss even though there was only so much I could do.

"Look," said the orange-faced man. "It was on her wrist when we were sitting at one of those fish restaurants by the seawall."

"Not while you were actually on the bus then?"

"No, but the tour advertises that all our needs will be met. I don't consider whether or not we are on the actual property of the company to be a criterion for fulfilling this contract." He had rehearsed his legal position.

"We are naturally interested in trying to help. Now, if you could perhaps tell us when you first noticed it missing."

"Like I said. At the restaurant. If that's what you call it."

Yes, I thought. We're also responsible for building and maintaining restaurants which conform to the standards of our most discriminating clients, and as an added service we will also make sure that the wind isn't too strong on the beach or that the seagulls don't cry off-key. "Did you register a complaint with the manager of the restaurant?"

"You mean the guy who was cooking? I don't think there *was* a manager."

"And you were, what? Eating and you noticed it gone?"

"Yes."

"But ... I have to be clear about this, sir. You didn't actually *see* any theft?"

"No, but it stands to reason. It was obviously a pickpocket. Now, what are you planning to do about it?"

"We *could* alert the police ..."

"Yes?"

"... But we have found in the past that complaints of this manner are met with less than satisfactory results. Have *you* alerted the police?"

"No. Since we are tourists in this country and you as tour guide are presumably more in touch with the customs and language of the place, I thought that the least you could do would be accept responsibility to help."

"Happy to do so. You don't actually know that it was a theft, though."

"Are you accusing me of lying?" There it was again.

"Not at all. Simply trying to get straight what happened."

He sighed heavily like I was an incredibly thick-headed student, and this was his hundredth time going through it.

"I'm *telling* you what happened."

"That you were sitting at a tuna restaurant, and found it missing?"

"That we were sitting at a restaurant and that it was stolen."

"But you didn't see it stolen."

"No. Obviously. If I'd seen it, it wouldn't have *been* stolen then. I would have stopped the thief."

With a karate chop to the neck, perhaps.

The fact that I was not who I said I was allowed me to be emotionally detached. It's one of the advantages of doing what I do. One of the reasons, I suppose, *why* I do it. If I'm too close, if there's too much at stake, I get confused and angry like everybody else.

I pursed my lips and said: "The only thing I can think of doing is to file a report when we get to Marrakech." Although that, I considered, might create problems. If he took me into the office as soon as we arrived, it could become complicated. I might have to get off at the rest stop before, if there was one, or escape as soon as I got off the bus in Marrakech.

He said: "Oh, sure." Like this is what he had come to expect. But he led his girl away and took a seat. On a hunch I walked down the aisle. And yes, I saw something under a seat in back. I approached, leant down, picked it up and walked back up the aisle.

"You were in a different seat coming out?" I asked.

"Oh, what?" said the orange-faced man. "We have to stay in the same seats? Is that it? I mean, My God, the bus is *half empty.*"

"No sir, I'm simply asking."

"Why?" He was making a fuss. The other tourists were starting to raise their eyebrows.

"This was on the floor back there," I said, and I held the bracelet out.

"Oh! You found it!" said the girl.

I gave it to her. "You must've left it behind. Happens all the time."

"Well. Thank you. You see? I *told* you it wasn't stolen," she said.

He didn't say anything, but he was offended. He had been made a fool of, and would be my enemy for life.

I walked to my seat, sat down and waited as the bus filled up. There would be about thirty of them, past the critical mass where a group of people become an audience. A captive audience, too, tired and open. Someone once told me that the Celtic word for "story" means literally "mile-shortener." I was just the man for it.

"All right," I said for my opening, "is everybody here? By which I mean, is there anybody you notice who is missing from when you rode out here this morning?" I waited. They looked around. "Sorry," I said in an aside to Sayeed. "I should have been given a list." He leant around and checked himself.

"That's it," he said, turned back, and closed the door. He started the bus, pulled out with a hiss, and drove out onto the road that ran along the beach away from Essaouira. I felt that old thrill I always get whenever I start a journey.

I stood up in the aisle holding onto the back of the two front seats, changing my weight with the sway of the bus, like the surfers on the waves we were passing.

"My name is Charles LeCastre, and I'll be your guide back to Marrakech. We hope you enjoyed your stay in Essaouira, formerly 'Mogador,' Phoenician colony, pirate port of the Barbary Coast, then a Portuguese, then a French Protectorate." They looked at me like: "What is this about?" And if I didn't come up with something quick I would lose them, which wouldn't be fatal because a real tour guide would not be expected to deliver a polished performance. But what else but duty gets you into your workday? Other things might happen after that, but that first step is always yours to take.

"We have just left the new part of town, and will soon be crossing the coastal range of hills, called here the 'Whaleback' or possibly 'Big Fish-Back' because of the shape." I looked around to the front, as we passed a milepost with Arabic writing which I didn't understand, and Arabic numbers which I did. "It is 438 kilometres to Marrakech," I said, "and will take 3 1/2 hours ..." I looked at Sayeed, who nodded agreement. I turned back and saw one orange face looking back at me narrowly. He had seen the milepost too and suspected that I was improvising. "That's according to the milepost we just passed," I said, and his face changed to disappointed that he hadn't caught me out. This could become a problem. If I was going to have to deal with facts, it was going to cramp my style. Best to get back onto the solid ground of fiction. I took a deep breath:

There's a story they tell about a lady who lived alone on the shore just south of here, and this was back when all this land, El Maghreb, was flat. She ate oysters she collected in the shallow water and threw a net for fish, and lived just above the tide-line in a hut made of driftwood.

Every year, though, there was a marauding band of brigands who swept in from the east and when she saw them coming she would always hide in the brush until they raided her house and stole everything they could. Then they would kick dirt onto the fire-pit, knock over her hut, and ride away. So she would have to rebuild, every year, and it had started to become tiresome.

One year she was hiding from them in the mouth of a small cave, watching the brigands destroy her home once again, and she heard a voice behind her. "What are you doing in my cave?" it said.

She jumped outside and turned around, and looked back in but couldn't see anything.

"Who are you?" said the lady.

"I am the Djinn who lives in this cave," said he. "Invite me out and I will give you three wishes."

Now the lady knew that a Djinn had to be invited out to escape his prison, and that whoever did so would indeed get three wishes, but once he'd granted those three wishes the Djinn was released from his bondage and could do terrible things, so it was always better to ignore the offer and continue doing the daily work that Fate had decreed for you, without supernatural and possibly diabolical interference. So she was about to just move away and avoid this place in the future, when she heard a shout and looked up to see the brigands, running towards her through the scrub yelling: "There she is! Get her!"

"Djinn, come out and grant me my three wishes," she said and the Djinn stepped out and said: "What will the first wish be, my lady?"

By this time the brigands were almost upon her. So, not having time to formulate a more careful wish, she said: "Stop the brigands." And with that the band of brigands stopped suddenly, some in mid-step, some with their scimitars over their heads ready to strike and with their war cries frozen in their throats.

"Would my lady like to make a second wish?" said the Djinn. And now the lady had time to think. The last wish should be that the Djinn return to his cave until he was invited out again, lest he be freed from bondage and do terrible things. So that meant she had one practical wish left. What would it be?

I paused, then dropped my storytelling tone. "If you look behind you," I said, "you will see the last view (I think it's the last) of Essaouira."

They all dutifully looked behind, then turned back to me, the spell broken. Not a smart storytelling move, but I found myself needing time to come up with that third question. I must be slipping: it was high time I got back into it. The bus took a lurch over a small hillock in the road and an idea occurred to me. "So where were we?" I said.

"The second wish," reminded the girl who was with the orange-faced man. He looked at her sourly.

"For my second wish ...," said the lady.

"Yes?" said the Djinn.

"Let me think," said the lady, then she thought to herself: What I would really like is that the brigands disappear and never come back and I'm left in peace on the shore. But that's three wishes. Perhaps if I put it in the form of one wish, like: "That events be so configured that ..." But she knew from all the stories of Djinns that the wish had to be as specific as possible, for any ambiguity whatsoever could be exploited by the Djinn, often causing bad things to happen. So she thought and thought and finally said:

"My second wish is that the coast be drawn back like the edge of a carpet to just in front of where I am standing." And the Djinn said: "So be it." And the ground rumbled and the surface of the earth pulled back, wrinkling up behind them these mountains which we are now crossing. The brigands, released from their spell of her previous wish, now found themselves splashing about in the deep ocean and the lady and the Djinn stood on the new shore.

"There," said the lady. "That should teach those brigands, and these new hills behind me should protect me from other tribes invading from the east and I will be left in peace."

"What's your third wish?" said the Djinn with a sigh, knowing what it would be.

"That you return to your cave," said the lady, "until some-one else invites you out." And the Djinn disappeared, and the lady started rebuilding her home for the last time.

I bowed.

"That was excellent," said the girl.

"Yes," said the orange-faced man, loud enough for everybody to hear. "Djinn stories are very popular in Arab culture." I may know a few stories, he implied, but he could actually explain their significance and history. An academic.

Why was he out to get me? Jealousy? I wasn't attracted to her at all. Maybe his enmity was partly caused by something as silly as my clothes.

Although everything I owned was either on my back or in my satchel on the seat beside me, my clothes themselves were impressive, and I could see how they might make him envious. I had bought them in Paris at a time when I had money to spend, in one of those camping stores behind the Musée de Cluny. They were ridiculously over-practical, full of grommets and carabineers in brass, with zipper vents for adapting to every sort of weather and, although many of the features were absurd and gimmicky, some of them did actually work well. Mainly though, they were the perfect costume. Expensive, as well as expensive-looking, they gave the impression that I was a wealthy man slumming it, vacationing for an indeterminate time in a simpler world. I might go hiking for the adventure, my clothes said, but I could always go to the bank and get more funds transferred to me. And because they were the only clothes I owned they were frayed satisfyingly, and because they were well-made, this improved them, as long as you kept them clean and pressed. I had been careful to lay them carefully under my mattress the last night I had slept in a room, because if you are homeless, you had better not look like it.

The Orange Man was wearing a sort of a cheaper version of what I was wearing, bought specially for the trip. They were still factory-creased, but although newer, they were less authentic. He hadn't put in the hours. Anybody could tell that I was the real thing and he was the second-hand man.

Which was odd, considering ...

And just then we passed the goat in the tree.

The schoolteacher said: "Look at that!" And we all looked outside the window where she pointed. On top of one of the argan trees was a goat, nibbling leaves. I'd seen them like this in postcards, but never in real life. I was the guide, however, and soon they would be looking back at me for information.

But the man with the orange face broke in. "I heard they *put* the goats up there," he said.

"Yes. A lot of people say that," I said, though it was the first time I'd heard of it. "But I myself am not sure. I suppose maybe one dry year, one particularly adventurous goat, kept by the rest of the herd from the juicier leaves at the bottom of the tree, climbed a particularly climbable tree, higher than the rest, and drew a crowd. Photos were taken, money changed hands. It was deemed a boon to the community, a traffic builder. So they maybe ... *encouraged* him the next day. That's just a theory."

"So it's a scam?"

"No. The goat really is up there. Would it be a less interesting display of balance if he was placed or if he climbed?" Or less than this balancing act I was performing?

"But we are being manipulated."

You have no idea. "If someone put them up there? Why?"

"They want us to believe the goat got there on its own."

The audience was on my side, as they always are when their entertainment is being spoiled. If you're going to heckle the comedian, you'd better be funnier than the guy on stage. I took a deep breath, and in what could be possibly interpreted as a parody of his academic tone I said: "If it is important to your appreciation of the goat-in-the-tree phenomenon that the goat be there without human aid, I am saying that I can't be sure. Since these are all *plantations* of trees, you could argue that if it wasn't for human intervention the trees themselves wouldn't be here, or indeed, that since the domestic goat in all its variety is the product of breeding and husband-ry stretching down from the dawn of mankind, goats *themselves*, as we know them, (at least the domestic kind) would not be around without human aid, and that we in a sense have created *them*."

But I wanted to get away from the podium and down to the campfire, away from argument and into story. "My view, for what it is worth, is not so much that we've had an impact on goats, but that *they've* had one on *us*. Or at least on me. (I have a dent in my shin to prove it.)" Which got me at laugh.

"Very funny," said the Orange Man. "But you haven't answered the question. Do they climb there, or are they put there?"

I don't know why I felt the desire to diminish him. And I told myself that I must watch it, lest I have contempt for the contemptuous. And just then I had a sudden clear vision of the way the devil works: not by eliminating good people, but by enlisting them.

I actually saw this as I was getting involved, and it let me see the point of not engaging. I thought, how much of everything is just this? How many people enslaved by not having the strength to let it slide?

Then I thought, there is a story in that.

We were coming down the far dry slope of the hills. Soon we would be through Chichaoua with its dogs, and the dry wadi with the shrubs in the bottom. Beyond that was real desert, and we would pass the outcrops of mountains to the south of us with nothing on the plain, and the passengers would fall silent as the bus hummed. Outside the window I saw a goatherd walking behind his herd on a hillside scattered with loose brown rock. The goats swarmed down the hill in front of him like foam in front of a breaking wave, the goatherd striding biblically behind with giant downhill strides, his staff waving in front of him like a prophet. I took a last look at him, and something real swam down the sunbeam into my eye and I started to tell them about it.

T WAS THE best story I had ever told. Like nothing I had ever heard before. They were attentive, indeed they were riveted, but I had told stories before that had done that to an audience. It fell together, each piece contributing to the whole, but although that was rare on the first telling, that had happened before to me as well. This story had something else. Somehow it described what it was like to be alive. They couldn't help but listen, then they nodded, agreeing.

Except the Orange Man. When I started telling it, he adopted an expression on his face like he was trying to bore holes in me with his eyes, but he only succeeded in presenting a model for my character in the story. He crossed his arms and frowned like a child sticking his fingers in his ears. Listening to me and accepting would mean that he would have to admit that the world may be arranged in some other way than he would have it. He was a careerist, in real life and in my story, and the politics of maintaining his position probably interfered with his ability with the work itself. Unless he had twice the energy or efficiency, how could he do both? The work, like everything else in his life, was just another brick on the step to the place where the world behaved as he wanted. That was all in the story, that was what was *feeding* the story, and the goatherd was in it too, and how they connected. It was also about how the meek shall inherit the earth. Not "the earth" in the sense of the world and everything in it, but in the sense of the soil itself, from which everything grows.

Something new had come into me and I no longer felt I had to engage, which I suppose was what the story was about as well, I realized, as I came to the end. I hoped I could remember it forever and not be distracted from what it said.

When I'd finished the Orange Man said: "Well, that's an old one." Which was untrue. But who am I to criticize? He could of course never have heard it before, but it was easy to believe that it was what he said. A good new story always feels like it's been here forever.

"I've never heard it before," said one of the ladies.

"Check out the Djemma el Fna when we get to back to Marrakech," he said. "Somebody'll be telling that one every night." The Djemma was a large square in the centre of Marrakech. Storytellers gathered there at night, along with sages, animal acts, anything that would draw a crowd. He was saying I'd stolen it.

"How do you know?" she said. He had engaged her.

"I study them," he said. "I am a Professor of Folklore."

Which was well played, I'll say that. But he wouldn't be a very good professor of folklore, I found myself thinking. No real scholar would lie about having heard my story before. This made me happy, sad to say, and I told myself that I should watch out for that as well.

We stopped for ten minutes at a roadside tourist shop with a restaurant. In the hall between the washrooms a fat little boy was stationed at a table, willing to take your money for the non-service he provided. Then there was more rock-strewn desert outside the window and finally we were into the vineyards on the outskirts of Marrakech, vines on rickety pergolas made from poles tied together, and more traffic on the road for the bus to move through: mopeds, donkey carts and pedestrians. The sun was going down, less obviously when I looked through the tinted windows of the passenger seats, but dusty, lovely and red when I turned and looked ahead through the clear windshield. Right now out of sight in front of us, the walls of the city would be glowing like an ember, but by the time we reached there it would be too dark to witness. Alongside the road now the top-floor windows of the apartment buildings winked gold, with single bulbs dispelling the shadows at street level. Between these buildings stood houses with unfinished top floors. If completed, they would be taxed, and so authority stops progress. All you can probably do is stay low.

Only as low as the ground, of course, but even there you can look for a crack in the mud to sprout through, send the root hairs out to feel for smaller hairline cracks again, thicken into roots, and crack the mud further and turn it into soil. I glimpsed a group of men sitting around a table in the hard light from a single bulb, leaning in and listening to a man near the centre. One of the listeners, somewhat apart from the rest, was leaning back in his chair, smoking and nodding, his waiter's jacket open at the neck. Then we passed, the vision was snatched from me, and the apartment buildings gave way to new palm trees along clean avenues, and we were in the Gueliz.

It was time to wrap it up. And this last story had to have a moral, the hardest kind of stories to make. The best way is just to lay the blocks in a row, then lay blocks on top of them, and if the foundations are strong, you could build something which would take the shape as you built, and needed only the faintest glimmer of inspiration, a sudden view of what that story had been so far, to sum the whole thing up, surprising and inevitable. But when you wanted to make a point, you were starting with a narrower field to draw from, and anything which didn't support that preordained shape had to be eliminated up front. Also, the ending never really surprised you, or them. The Muse got bored.

Still, it had to be done. "One last story," I said. I couldn't see their faces in the dark now, but felt their attention turn towards me.

It's about when I was a waiter in a restaurant near here. All day, six days a week I would serve tables in a small cafe off the Boulevard Mohammed Cinq. I made very little money, but I was happy and occupied.

The only thing which disturbed me was something I started to notice about my customers. No matter how excellent or not I was at my job, some people would tip me, and others would not. It wasn't the money, understand, it was that there didn't seem to be any pattern to their behaviour. Kind-looking people who felt apologetic at asking for any food at all, and who you thought would be generous, left without leaving anything, and nasty demanding boors who made your life miserable would leave whole bills of large denomination fluttering on the table cloth. I devised theories and tried to guess how the next customer would tip, but every theory and guess I made was inevitably proven wrong by the next customer. It started as a pass-time and became an obsession.

One day, into the restaurant came a man like a gathering storm, sullen, angry and brooding. He sat down with a thump at a table I hadn't yet cleared from the customer who had just left, then he leant around in the chair looking for service and, when I went to clean up the table, he shamelessly pocketed the tip that had been left by the previous customer, with a nonchalant air which, if challenged, he could claim was thoughtlessness on his part. There would be trouble with this one. He managed to look annoyed by my ministrations and after I'd finished, when I asked him what he would like, he made me wait a good long time before he decided on something, then cancelled that order, asked for something else, cancelled that, and finally decided on mint tea, like there was nothing else that this restaurant could probably safely produce. Then, when I returned with his order, he changed his mind again and asked for just coffee.

I went back behind the counter, took the espresso basket, filled it with coffee, tamped it down and squeezed the coffee in, wishing it was that customer's brains. Then I fitted the basket below the steam valve and pulled it tight like a tourniquet around the customer's neck, and when the little light turned off, indicating that enough of a head of steam had built up, I cranked the switch, pretending it was the customer's nose.

I took a deep breath and brought the customer his coffee with a smile but just as I started to place it in front of him, he reached greedily for it and knocked the cup off the saucer, immediately casting an accusing glance at me as though it was my fault.

So I apologized, went to get another place setting, cleaned up, and when I returned with a new coffee, the customer was standing holding the corner of his jacket where there was a stain which was easily three days old but which he claimed loudly had been caused when I spilled it.

Now, I knew that I hadn't made the stain, and knew that whatever I did, the customer was going to blame me, and I thought what should I do? The customer (who by the smell of his breath I could tell had been drinking) was starting to complain in a loud voice, asking what sort of a restaurant was this? And from his wounded tone, although what he was saying was absolutely untrue, other customers were starting to feel uncomfortable.

"I am extremely sorry," I said, for you cannot meet anger with anger. "I will personally take care of the jacket, and arrange that you should have a free meal as well."

So I took his jacket and ordered the meal and, while the awful customer waited to be fed, I went three doors away to a large hotel off the Boulevard where a friend worked and got him to rush a cleaning job, and an hour later, after the customer had eaten his large free meal and retrieved his jacket, he got up and departed, leaving, of course, no tip ...

The bus turned three times and came to a halt with a hiss. When the driver turned off the engine the silence rang. I had to wrap up.

... Then the awful customer walked out of the restaurant, burped, and was run over by a tour bus from Essaouira, which was full of exactly the opposite type of customer, all people who were generous, kind and huge tippers. Thank you.

My audience, who I could now see by the light of the streetlamp we had pulled under, applauded, except of course the Orange Man. His girl started to, but stopped when she caught a look from him. Sayeed rubbed his eyes, then opened the door and stepped out to get the baggage onto the sidewalk from the compartment under the side of the bus. He pulled out the few bags and souvenirs, lay them on the sidewalk and I followed and stood by the door. Where we had stopped was beside a storefront with the company logo painted on the window.

First off was the lady in the front seat.

"Thank you," she said. "That was most interesting."

I didn't say anything, just smiled and nodded, waiting patiently. She took the hint, rummaged in her purse, and gave me a euro. Not bad. The next man gave me another, and now that the protocol was established I could see the people who were filed behind in the bus, reaching in their pockets or asking those they were with for change to give me. I could afford to adopt my "This-is-really-not-necessary" look as I took their money. The Orange Man came out, whispering out of the side of his mouth to his girl, and of course he didn't leave a tip. "Watch you don't get run over," I said. He turned to see if I was taking a parting jab at him but there was only concern on my face. Then the moped I had seen, carrying what looked like a whole family and all their possessions, buzzed toward him like a hornet and he turned to see it and stepped back, so was almost, in fact, run over. He moved off down the sidewalk without looking back, shaking his girl off his arm. My parting view of them was as they were leaving around the corner, both of them angry, he at me, she at him.

"Thank you. Thank you," I said to the other customers as they filed off, handing me change. It was the expected thing now. Quite a haul by the time the final customer picked up his shopping bag and walked off.

"Half of this is yours," I said to Sayeed.

"Thank you," he said, surprised.

Knock and the door shall be opened unto you. "I slept in one of those once," I said, looking at the baggage compartment. He was eyeing the change in his hand, then he looked up, caught my eye and made a decision.

"We park it here tonight," he said. "I'll tell them you're a customer, so you can use the washroom in the office."

We entered, and he went over to the counter. "Sharon," he said, "is it all right if he uses the washroom?"

"Go ahead." And I nodded to her and went in.

When I came out he was still talking to her. "Don't forget your luggage," he said, and I followed him out to the bus, he opened the compartment, glanced around to see that nobody was watching, and then he nodded to me. I climbed in. "I'll leave it open a crack," he said. "Sleep well."

It wasn't bad accommodation at all. Dry, raised, clean, and with no danger of rats nibbling your toes. I took my few clothes out of my satchel, and changed my underwear and socks. Then I wrapped my shoes in a plastic bag for a pillow, stretched out, and tossed and turned until I figured out how to stuff my spare socks into my pockets so they would cushion my hips if I rolled. I discovered that the most comfortable position was to lie like a mummy with my arms across my chest.

I found myself thinking what was the point of all this? Which is dangerous. But once you're thinking about something, you can't just switch it off. The only thing you can do is steer it away, or include it.

So. Whoever or whatever is in charge of things, I thought, well, that's sacred. Everybody wants things to be better, and that all starts with you and the people around you. I should first try to be grateful for the good things that happened today, the goat brochettes, the wine, the good people on the bus who listened, and all those lovely tips at the end of the journey. Good things had happened. And, if only in my own mind, I might as well make up to anybody who I think has wronged me, because God knows I've done some things to people which probably need being made up to as well. So let's call it a draw, Whoever or Whatever's in charge. And please don't let me fall into that crippling hatred, because if I do, I'll not be doing any good to anybody, least of all myself. That's how things can get better, and that's the only thing that matters, and probably ever will.

And it seemed to me that everything meant something again. I knew what I had to do, or at least how to behave when whatever happened. And then I fell asleep easily. Consciousness is keeping three balls in the air. Sleep is just letting them fall.

Around four in the morning it started to get cool and I awoke, rearranged my padding and slept until about seven, when pink light flooded in the crack under the door. I gathered my things. Three pairs of socks, three pairs underwear, bathing suit, two shirts, razor, sewing kit, soap and toothbrush. I folded them neatly away into my satchel. Then, waiting until there was no sound on the street, I opened the door, slipped out and stood on the sidewalk. A Berber lady looked at me as she passed but didn't register surprise. It wasn't her business. I started down the street in the opposite direction, looking for a café I could afford with a toilet I could use. I bought a loaf of bread in a small grocery store, broke it in two and put it in the side pockets of my satchel. The sun was rising and the street was starting to hum like a meadow. I was still walking around in the afterglow of my previous night's thoughts, and I wondered if I could behave in the way they dictated but still survive. And as it turned out I almost immediately found myself compromising.

I rounded a walled enclosure past some scaffolding and came upon the arched driveway of a new hotel. There was a booth for a doorman, but nobody was guarding the gate. I caught my reflection in the glass door and decided I could pass, so I walked inside, nodded at the man behind the desk like he should recognize me and continued walking through the lobby. Straight hallways ran off from either side and everything was trimmed in exotic wood, and there were glass cases with works of art and sculpture which you could purchase if you were burdened with altogether too much money. The scaffolding had fooled me. This was a classy hotel, almost out of my league. But that might work in my favour: it might well be more impersonal. I kept up my purposeful stride straight through out to the bright courtyard. Palm trees stood in large pots back from a swimming pool which trembled in the middle like a square of turquoise jelly. They were just opening the poolside café.

I ordered a coffee, then went back into the lobby to a rack on the wall where I had seen stacked brochures suggesting such things as day trips to the high Atlas and Azzazoute. I took five or six cheaply printed sheets advertising karaoke night at a disco, went out to the courtyard again, sat down where my coffee had arrived and looked at the receipt. The only way it would be worth as much as they were asking was if each coffee bean was individually flown in from Brazil by private jet. I would have to make it last. I took my pencil and sharpener out of my shirt pocket, laid out one of the sheets as though I was planning my business itinerary for the day, and started to write on its blank side everything that had happened to me since yesterday. One of the ways to appear that you belong is to look busy.

WROTE UNTIL about ten o'clock, when hotel guests were starting to come onto the patio. I folded my sheets into my inside pocket, finished the last thimbleful of coffee, paid, then asked the whereabouts of the washroom which turned out to be through a doorway on the other side of the pool.

Nobody was in the washroom. I quickly brushed my teeth, listened for approaching steps, then took out my socks and underwear and washed them in the sink with my rapidly diminishing bar of soap. If I came across a maid with her cleaning cart, I might ask for some of the complimentary soap that hotels like this give out to real guests.

I changed into my bathing suit, put everything back into my miraculous satchel, and folding my jacket over my arm, I walked back out to the pool. I lay my jacket on an empty lawn chair, stepped out of my shoes, and placed the wet socks and underwear out of sight under the chair in a sunbeam. I walked around to the steps into the pool and took my time entering the water, then swimming across and back. I tried floating, but I wasn't as buoyant as in the ocean at Essaouira, and here there was a smell of too much chlorine. I reflected how it was that, whenever I rose in society, things became more uncomfortable. Not to complain though: it was still pretty good here.

A hotel guest with a towel over his shoulder came into the courtyard and entered the pool from the opposite side. After a seemly amount of time I pulled myself out of the water and sat on the edge with my shins and feet still in. Then I climbed completely out, walked over to my lawn chair, and checked how my laundry was doing. It was almost dry and I rearranged it so that the sunbeam would fall on it more directly, then lay down on the lawn chair and fell asleep. I dreamt something quick and vicious and woke up with the sense of someone looming over me.

"Excuse me, sir," said a hotel employee. "Are you staying here?"

What I should have said was simply "yes," but he had caught me just waking up, and I was not at my best. "No. Yes. That is ..."

"Sir?"

"I was just about to ... Yes. There was a mix-up at the desk. That's why I was swimming."

"Oh?"

My thoughts started shuffling into some sort of order. "I told them I'd be staying tonight and they said I couldn't check in yet, for some reason. They said if I would like to wait, I could go for a swim."

"Very good sir," he said, and he left to the lobby, where he would be asking questions.

It was time to move. I pulled my pants on over my bathing suit and packed my underwear and socks, which were now bone dry.

A new couple on the far side of the pool had stopped talking and were looking at me. As I did up my shirt, I smiled at them broadly and they turned back and started talking to each other again. I put the satchel over my shoulder, straightened my clothes, took a few euros out of my pocket, and jangled them in my hand like a talisman. I walked around the pool and into the lobby holding the tourist brochures in my other hand like an actor's prop. I saw the man who had awoken me waiting his turn to talk to the man behind the desk and I went over to him, jangled the coins in my hand like a nervous habit, and smiled a composed smile as he turned towards me.

"Sorry about that," I said. "I fell asleep. I'm staying at the Mamounia but I was looking for some place cheaper. I was thinking I'll stay here tonight."

"Very good sir. Can we check you in?"

"I'll have to get my luggage first," I said.

"We could send someone over for that."

I looked at him. He looked back. I pocketed the change. If he wasn't going to accept my story I certainly wasn't going to leave him a tip.

"No," I said, "the walk will do me good." And I swung out the door and strode quickly away. I had the impression that he followed me to the door and watched me until I was out of sight.

The first chance I got, I ducked around a corner into a back street. It was shadier there, and I didn't want to be in the open. He'd shaken me.

I walked quickly up the street past a walled garden, and remembered that the Arabic word for "Garden" is "Paradise." A rag-picker drove his donkey cart towards me and smiled. I smiled back, slowed my walking and started to breathe more evenly. I came to a wider boulevard with the city walls on the other side. I crossed, then walked up to and through the Bab Doukkala into the medina. The sound of traffic was instantly no more.

In a ryad on one side, a hard-looking European woman watched from the terrace, and on the other end of the street two girls ran out of a school and started home. I passed another ryad with a dirt floor in the courtyard and a boy crouched over a foot-lathe bowing back and forth a tube of whirling thuya wood. Across from a small mosque I found a place to sit and have some mint tea.

"I don't want to buy anything else," I said to the man who ran things. "Just tea, and to sit here for a while. If it starts getting crowded, I'll move along."

Best to make things clear from the start. And sure enough, now I was starting to feel better.

"Of course, of course," he said. "Sit." It was why he was here, only to serve. A man has to earn a living, but you are a human being too, not a braying donkey who only wants, wants, wants.

He brought me tea and sat down as well. I was his only customer. "The crowds are not what they used to be," he said apologetically. We both looked at the sun slanting on the door of the mosque across the street.

"Crowds can bring problems too," I said.

"Yes," he said. "We should be grateful for the quiet moments."

I nodded. Maybe everything *was* possible. I started to remember again what I had been thinking the night before about making things better. I was tired of the game. I had a hundred euros in my pocket but everything I owned was on my back.

But it wasn't dire. Even if I had been found out at the hotel, what really was at stake? Public embarrassment, but probably not prison, though I couldn't say that for sure. After all, this was a foreign country.

The door of the mosque opened and a man came out, followed by another, and then, after a pause, the rest of the devout from the neighbourhood. My friend stood up in expectation of possible business, back to the grind. The street started to fill up, and then a large well-fed cop in khakis walked slowly up out of the souks and through the crowd. People didn't acknowledge him, just busied themselves with looking elsewhere or talking with more concentration to each other until he passed. And when he was out of sight they resumed normal relaxed activity, like songbirds after a falcon has flown overhead. I glimpsed something awful in my mind, a vision of a world where uniforms rule. And how lonely he must feel in that uniform. Wherever he went, people innocently occupying themselves with something else. Like a nightmare I used to have, where everybody was too busy to listen to me.

I felt something approaching in my mind, that familiar nervousness whenever a good one comes along, some group of ideas which had to be expressed soon because they don't keep.

It would be a political story, though. Dangerous. Maybe as an animal story it might be acceptable. *"There once was a falcon and a flock of doves ..."*

But it was probably not the kind of story you could tell for instance in the Djemma without word getting around. You might be closed down and dragged away, maybe even thrown in prison and beaten up.

I thought I should pay a visit to the French Embassy, down by the Koutoubia, just in case. I could make my presence known, get the name of someone who would potentially help if things went wrong. Then if I screwed up too badly, the worst that could happen would be to have to ask them for help, and then, after being sternly condescended to for a while, I would be transported back to France. In my mind I came up against a memory, a jab of humiliation from back in Paris, but I shoved it away. I had left Paris with my eyes open, I had known what I was doing, and it was nice not to have any deadlines, truth to tell, or at least no deadlines but the big one. To be able to follow the Muse where she wanted to go, not where commerce said she should, that is a privilege, so of course it takes sacrifice. The good stuff is more than just filling in the blanks. And these last two days she had been smiling on me. Please stay, Muse. Life has no point without you.

When I judged that it was time for things to start happening in the Djemma, I paid for the tea and said goodbye to my friend. I walked to the end of the street and turned into the souks, walked down a slight grade past stalls where they sold stringed instruments, then wooden bowls, then past the woodworkers, leather-workers, fruit and vegetable vendors and slipper makers. The quality and service generally got worse the closer you got to the Djemma, where the day tourists got off buses, poked their noses in and bought a souvenir or two. I walked straight through without looking because I knew that if you stayed and admired anything, there would be that two minutes of banter about the object, turning suddenly to anger at wasting their time if the sale was not made, an emotional manipulation to keep you engaged. Business at its core. How bad do you want this? How much can you afford? How much is it worth? The unimaginably complicated system of barter, profit and loss, getting and spending ...

Then I lost my way. I wasn't paying attention and was eddied into an alley where they sold hammered brass plates and copper sinks. I asked the way to the Djemma and a boy who looked as though he had been positioned there for exactly this purpose led me back to where I had taken the wrong turn. Here my clothing put me at a disadvantage: I looked wealthier than I was. I gave him 20 dirhams and thanked him, and he seemed satisfied. I continued down the wider thoroughfare, a sloping street with a bamboo matting roof. I joined another wider open street where they sold desert roses and fossilized sea snails, and came out onto the Djemma just as it was starting to bounce and hop.

The sounds of tambourines and gas generators increased in volume as I walked into the moving crowd. Through the haze of cooking smoke and exhaust the sun reddened and set. And with the pulse of the Djemma something started to thrum in me, like the sympathetic strings on a sitar. I walked to the row of orange-juice stands, and then around the entire square, moving with the current of the crowd. In the eddies of this current, monkey acts, fife-and-drum musicians, acrobats and sages performed. A man with a beat-up falcon on a rug worked the slim crowd around him. Water carriers came up to me and offered me drink. Music played, stories told, wisdom dispensed, sooths said.

The Djemma el Fna was probably the hardest place in the world to play the angles. Since the time that Marrakech was a crossroads in the desert, every angle ever devised had been played and developed and included into a tradition of angle-playing, to be sharpened and improved by future generations of angle-players. So it is with a certain amount of pride that I tell you that I believe I discovered a new one.

STOUT, IMPOSING lady in black, a widow wearing a hijab but no veil, was holding in thrall thirty young men around her with a story she was telling. The youngest boy of all had tentatively snuck in front, wondering if he'd catch hell for being there. She registered my arrival at the back of the crowd, but didn't break her rhythm. It was a remarkable rhythm. She had the gift. I didn't understand a thing she said, but I understood what she was doing. I knew her. I *was* her.

She said something, the audience reacted, she gestured with her hand like a Madonna. Her audience nodded again: yes, it's like that. And the rhythm of her speech nourished the reaction of her audience. They laughed a short laugh of surprise and recognition. We aren't hearing a story now, we're in the story itself. And so she made the platform to step onto. She adjusted her wide sleeve over her forearm as though to make the step up, onto a higher viewpoint to put the next brick in the stair. Higher again. Now she had her own material to draw on, arrange what she already had into a new configuration. It won't happen, it can't happen, something better than both happened. Now what? I moved over behind the crescent of people, mostly boys and young men, sitting in front and standing behind.

And that was when I saw the girl.

She was fiddling with a small recording device. She gave it a smack like it was a pet which had nipped her, then she gave up trying to fix it, and just listened, frowning. She was both cute and alone. I thought she was becoming aware of my presence so I looked straight ahead and re-acted to the story the widow was telling. I said "Ooo" when the audience did, laughed when they laughed. "That was a good one," I said after a big laugh, and smiled at her. Another guy was moving in from the other side, she caught a glimpse of him out of the corner of her eye, and moved closer to me. Proper attire will win it for you every time.

An older tourist couple was standing on my other side. "What's she saying?" asked the wife.

"It's a story about a man and his two sons," I said.

"Come on, dear," said the husband, and they moved off. When I turned back, the girl with the tape recorder was looking at me with curiosity. It seemed to me that she had come to some sort of decision.

"I wish *I* knew what she was saying," she said.

"Do you want me to translate?" I offered.

She looked at me, considering, then decided. "Yes. Please. OK."

"This one's coming to an end, " I said. "We'll wait for the next."

"OK."

I smiled at her. She was here for more than mere touristic interest. There was something professional about her. "University?" I asked.

"Yes. I ..."

"Ah. Here it comes ..." I interrupted her, because the widow had started again. The audience quieted down. I let the widow speak for a bit, then said:

This was a long time ago. So long I can hardly say. Before cars, before mopeds, when the only way to get around was by walking, or by camel. Djoha had two new camels he was very proud of.

A friend of his met him and said: "Djoha, what lovely animals! I would like to buy one."

"Well," said Djoha, "as much as I would like to sell you one, I would like to keep both."

"But, Djoha," said the friend, "why would you need two camels?"

"One to carry things," said Djoha.

"And the other?" asked the friend ...

Whatever the widow had said now made the crowd laugh, and I had to think fast.

... And the other to carry things back.

"Not a very good one," I said, "but she has a way of saying it." This could be trickier than I thought.

"What's happening now?" said the girl with the tape recorder.

"Intermission," I said. The crowd settled down.

The girl fiddled with her recorder and drew out a microphone.

"They may take it badly if you record them," I said, which was true. They had it right, these people. It can steal your soul.

"I can pay."

"That will certainly help."

"Would you translate the next one for me into the microphone? If I can get this damn machine working?"

"Certainly," I said. "Shall we say, what? 200 euros?" A vast amount by my standards, but she seemed to have money. That tape recorder couldn't have been cheap.

She said: "Yes," a little bit shocked, but I had said it innocently, as though that was the common fee for us simultaneous translators, and she reached into her purse.

I stopped her, put my hand on her forearm, which was strong and warm.

"Afterwards," I said, "and only if you're satisfied." She smiled. Nice smile. "Now. Can I help with that recorder?"

"Please do," she said, and, silly girl, she handed it to me, a complete stranger.

"I'm good with these sorts of things," I said which might have been the biggest lie so far.

It was digital and modern. I started pushing buttons. One button turned everything off. I pushed another, it paused, then a small LED screen lit up and a row of tiny lights sprang into life. At one corner of the screen an image of a microphone highlighted. I pushed "enter". Abracadabra. A light in the corner blinked on and off, a crude animation of a tape recorder appeared and played. When I said "Hello? Hello?" into the microphone, a digital line in the tiny screen buckled and peaked. "There," I said. We were rolling.

The widow straightened up and moved to her spot to indicate that she was about to start, and the crowd shut up and looked at her. I nodded at her, she acknowledged my nod like she was including us, then, without breaking the thread between herself and the rest of her audience, she glanced at a man to her side who looked around and saw us. We'd be getting a visit later. I looked back at him and nodded like I understood, which I did. There would be some business to take care of after the story was finished.

I gave back the recorder to the girl and she held the microphone to me as I pretended to translate. The fact that I didn't understand the words was not important. I understood the rhythm. The widow's voice rose and fell like the music around us in the Djemma.

"It's about a man who liked money," I said. (I almost said "who liked meaning," but this was easier. Anyhow, I was committed now.)

"Oh?" said the girl, now a professional.

"Yes. He has heard about a cave in the desert where there is supposed to be gold."

He left his village and crossed the wadi and crossed the desert and climbed up the mountain to the cave, and the door was blocked by a large boulder.

A little laugh from the crowd at what she said made me have to justify it in my story.

"Oh Large Boulder! Why are you standing between me and the money?"

Another laugh.

But the boulder didn't answer.

The widow got serious and so did I. This might be a change of mood, or merely a set-up. All I could do was fill in a likely picture.

He looked around the edges of the boulder to see if there was a way in, then stood on his toes to see if he could crawl over it into the cave where the money was.

The widow stamped her foot.

He stamped his foot in frustration. Then he prayed to Allah to remove the boulder with a bolt of lightning, but the boulder stayed put. And then he asked Allah why did He put the boulder there?

The widow paused, gathered her wits and adjusted her robes, shrugged her shoulder to pull the cloth of her sleeve over her forearm. She started back into her story, building her rhythms. I started back into mine.

As he was standing there, a mouse appeared from under the rock, poking his head from out of a hole. "Hey," said the old man. "Can you get into the cave?"

The widow said something. Her audience laughed.

"Yes," said the mouse. "But I don't think you'd fit."
"Is there a box in there?"
"There are two boxes," said the mouse.
Two, thought the man. I will be richer than I thought!
And the mouse thought: What would he want those boxes for? I have opened both and there is one that was full of grain which I finished, and the other is full of shiny metal discs which you can't eat.

I cannot say it was shaping up into one of my best stories, but I was working under difficult conditions, which I took as a challenge, not an impediment. Walk across a smooth floor and only the mind which is smooth as the floor will be interested. But have an earthquake rumble and crack the floor in front of the walker, and you can't take your eyes off it. It pays to have stumbling blocks.

So I had to wait till the widow stopped talking, hear the reaction, and tailor my lines to some credible twist in the story which would create such a reaction. I wasn't working the same crowd as her. I wasn't working a crowd at all, just the girl with the recorder. But it got my heart pumping in a way I hadn't experienced while performing in quite a while.

So the mouse said: "Why should I do this for you?"

And the old man said: "I will give you some of the gold if you do."

"Gold? Is that what you call it?" said the mouse. "Those shiny discs you can't eat?"

"Yes," said the man, "but they are worthless." For he saw the mouse did not value it.

And the mouse thought: Why does he want what you can't eat?

"I will tell you what I will do," said the mouse. "If you go back and get me a bag of grain, I will give you this gold which you seem to want so much."

"I don't really want it," said the man. "My daughter likes shiny trinkets and I thought I would bring some back to amuse her."

"I will go and get the gold," said the mouse. "You go and get the grain." And the mouse went back into the cave and the man went to get the grain, down the mountain and across the desert and over the wadi and into the village.

The widow paused.

"Well I want to know what happens next," said the girl with the tape recorder.

"Me too," I said, which was honest, at least. I found myself wanting to tell the truth to her, but before I could examine this thought, the widow continued. Business first. Then I'd make it right.

As the man walked away he thought: After all, what is value? The mouse wants grain. I want gold. They are both the same in the eyes of Allah. Why do we have to lie to each other to get what we want? What Devil arranged the world so that I just can't say: You have gold, I have grain. If you have no use for what you have, give it to someone who does? Then he thought:

Why am I thinking this? I have business to do. And he went to a house where a grain merchant lived.

"I can give you gold tomorrow if you give me some grain today," he said.

"Why should I believe you?" said the grain merchant.

"Because I am an honourable man," said the old man.

"You are many things, old man," said the grain merchant, "but 'honourable' is not one of them. Remember when you sold me that donkey, and then the donkey went blind?"

"I didn't know he would go blind!" said the old man.

"So you said, but you bought it from your cousin whose donkeys had all gone blind except for this one."

"Ah, that cousin of mine!" said the old man. "He sold me that donkey knowing it would go blind. And I paid full price for it. And sold it to you at a loss."

"You knew the donkey would go blind, old man. You bought it cheap because you knew it would, and your cousin knew it as well. How can you say you are an honourable man! Were you honourable when you sold me that donkey? Were you honourable, just now, when you told me you didn't know the donkey would go blind? No! You are a dishonourable old man and if I give you grain you will take it then not pay for it." And with that the grain merchant threw up his hands and moved away, then turned back. "If I give you this grain, and you do not pay me tomorrow, I will be out of both money and grain, so I will give you some old grain which has not been cleaned, and is of very little use to me, as no one will buy it and I will not eat it. That way if you do not pay me, I will not be out much. Deal?"

"Deal," said the old man who took the grain and started back out of the village and over the wadi and across the desert and up the mountain to the cave, grumbling and thinking: *What right had that grain merchant to call me dishonourable? He only said that to pass off some old grain on me. Really, I* should trade the grain for the gold and not pay him for the grain. That would serve him right for calling me names!

When he reached the cave, the mouse was waiting for him outside his hole with one gold coin lying in front of him. "Is that all?" said the old man.

"No," said the mouse. "There is more, but you must give me some grain first."

"Why don't you give me all the gold and I will give you all the grain? To save time."

"Time," said the mouse, "is what we both have. And only so much, and we don't know how much. In this way we are the same."

"Thank you for the lesson in philosophy," said the old man. "But why not do it my way?"

"Because," said the mouse, "I've heard that you were dis-honourable."

"Who told you that?"

"A rock dove," said the mouse. "He overheard you talk to the grain merchant, and he flew here ahead of you to tell me."

"That rock dove is a liar."

"But if you are a liar, that means he is not."

"But if he is, then I am not," said the old man.

"But he has never lied to me before," said the mouse.

"And have I?" said the old man.

"I have no way of knowing," said the mouse. "But your reputation flies ahead of you."

Oh that reputation! thought the Old Man. I sold a donkey and it went blind. I did not make it go blind. I did not know it would go blind!

And in truth, the old man did not know it would go blind. He suspected it would go blind, he bought it at a low price on the grounds that it would probably go blind. But he did not know it. Only Allah knew that. Did he have to believe he was more knowledgeable than Allah to be honourable in this world?

And thinking this comfortable thought of how the burden of his goodness weighed on his shoulders in this evil world, his eye caught the glint of the gold coin, winking in the sun.

"Oh, all right," said the man, stamping his foot in frustration and shaking his fist. And he reached into the bag and grabbed a handful of grain. "There, you robber! Something you can eat, for something you cannot eat, which merely shines and has no value." And he took the coin and bit it.

And the mouse thought: What a strange animal who tries to eat what he says cannot be eaten.

"Give me another," said the old man. And the mouse went in and rolled out another coin, and the old man gave the mouse another handful of grain. And so on until the old man had all the gold, and the mouse had all the grain.

And the old man left and went down the mountain and on the way back across the desert he thought: Silly mouse! He didn't know what he had! And all it cost me was a bag of old grain.

And inside his cave, the mouse thought: Silly old man! All it cost me was some useless shiny metal!

And here the widow said something and ended, and her audience said "ah!" and looked at each other and nodded. So I had to end my story as well.

But the mouse was right because a dust storm came up and the old man lost his way in the desert, and the weight of the gold he couldn't eat but which he couldn't let go of, weighed him down, and he died.

And the girl nodded and turned off the recorder.

"Satisfied?" I said.

"Yes. Two hundred euros, was it?"

"Yes," I said. "And I'd better watch it or it will weigh me down and I will die on my way home."

She smiled. "Would you like to go for some mint tea?" she said.

"Yes," I said, "but I should give half of this to the widow."

"Oh," she said. "No. That's for you. There's another two hundred for her."

I resisted the temptation to jump in the air and hoot with joy. She reached into her purse and took some more money out, not something you should really do in a public place in Marrakech. She obviously needed my protection.

The man to whom the widow had signalled was standing beside me now, ready to get nasty if the situation demanded it, but not wanting to, it seemed to me.

"This is for you," I said immediately, and she handed him two hundred euros. He was stunned into pacification by the amount. The answer to world peace.

Then I saw something in his face which told me he was somebody I could do business with. If you look at the faces of people at a casino, when somebody wins, the look of surprise at good luck is replaced almost immediately with the possibility of getting more. But it seemed to me that he took some time to consider his luck and be grateful. "Thank you," he said, and smiled a quick remarkable smile. And that's how long it takes to make a friend. I said I'd see him again, and he said he hoped so.

I turned to the girl. "You were suggesting tea?"

"Yes. There's a place I like," she said, and led me through the crowd to one of the restaurants on the edge of the Djemma. We walked up to the second floor balcony and sat down overlooking the madness. The Djemma was one huge tambourine, beating rhythms which shifted from one into another as you listened, and the sun was down now and the sky above where it had set was lilac and orange. The Koutoubia was silhouetted over the trees, its top turret floodlit.

"Thank you," I said when tea was ordered, meaning that since she'd invited, she was paying.

"That's all right," she said. "I liked that story of yours."

"Of theirs, you mean," I said.

"How many languages do you speak?" she said.

"Apart from French? Arabic, of course."

"Of course," she said, with an odd smile which I took to mean that she was observing an unknown species, a natural linguist.

I held out my hand and counted off some more. "And English. And Norwegian, and Icelandic, and Russian." The problem with doing what I do is that sometimes it's hard to stop.

"Oh. *I* speak Russian," she said.

Oops. "That's my worst," I said.

"Drazvuchy. Kak voi pavayechek, " she continued. "That's all I know."

And I started breathing again. "Very nice accent all the same, " I said. "And now I have a question for you. What are the recordings for?"

"Fieldwork. Folklore."

"Oh? I just ran into somebody else who did that."

"Not surprising," she said. "There's a big conference in town." She looked sour for a moment, then snapped out of it. "We're supposed to be collecting some examples of different types of stories."

"Oh? How many types are there?"

"I guess that's one of the things we're hoping to find out."

"What for?"

Her eyes snapped with a sudden flash of frustration. "So we can get more funding to continue collecting stories," she said. Then she calmed down and sighed. "Or you could say to try and quantify an important part of culture and increase the sum of human knowledge. Or provide the tools by which we can learn better the art of narration and so be able to communicate with each other better. But no. Honestly? The reason we do it is to get funding to go on another junket. Sounds kind of pointless, doesn't it?"

"You here alone?" I asked.

"Apparently," she said and her eyes flashed again. She had been left to do somebody else's job.

"But there are others here *with* you."

"Not out on the square where they could be some use. No. They're shopping, or smoking hashish. Or generally stealing from the institution which is their reason for being here ... Oh well. No need to air my dirty laundry."

"I once went to a children's book fair in Tours," I said.

"That's where *I'm* from," she said, looking up. I thought I had heard that in her accent.

"Really? Well well. Anyway, there was one publisher."

He was famous. No one knew why. All he did was fly around to publishing conferences giving his speeches. But this was not his real talent. His real talent was climbing. He had a nose for finding the man in the position most beneficial to him, then attaching himself to him, introducing him to someone else, but only if that person was important to his own advancement.

"You know the type."

"Oh yes."

He'd get up in the morning, then he'd breakfast with so-and-so and find out what so-and-so could do for him and what he could do for so-and-so. Organized an invitation to some other person important to both him and whoever he was now acting as liaison for. He played his opportunities like a chess master. Gave speeches written on the spot, without any notes. Became a known quantity in the world of French Publishing. Showed up in government sponsored events to present Modern Classics in school. Appeared and was photographed with politicians when organizations received money. Flew to Dubai to give a consultation. Was hired to speak to foreign diplomats in China. Racked up air-miles and spent them to send himself to other get-togethers important to his career in other parts of the world. Lived in hotels.

Her eye started to wander. I was describing the world she was trying to leave. The story needed a jolt.

Then over the horizon there loomed a job, a valued plum of a job, with power and money and perks galore, an opportunity of enormous possibilities: Minister of Literacy in a newly formed department in government. And although the manoeuvrings for it, between him and a lady who had written a well-regarded novel, were intricate and lengthy, I will only say that the decision as to who would get the job came down to one after-dinner speech. The lady novelist gave a good enough talk, but his was a barn-burner. He played the room like a cello. He talked about the duty of the people who did this important work and the honour of even being considered for the post. And although anyone who worked with him knew he never did anything but charm people and delegate others to do any real work, when they heard him speak they thought, he's the one. They believed it because as he spoke he believed it. And three days later he got the job as minister in charge of literacy.

"Typical."
     "But wait."

On the morning of the first day at his new office, with his staff waiting for him, he was a half hour late. They called his room. No answer. They became worried. They went to the hotel where he was staying. The man at the desk said they hadn't seen him all morning. They called his room but nobody picked up the phone. The Hotel Manager went to his door, knocked and there was still no answer. The Manager put his master key into the lock and, calling the man's name, opened the door and found him there, hanging from the velvet curtain rope which he had tied around the chandelier. There was no suicide note.

When they contacted his family and pieced together why, they concluded that it had something to do with the fact that, although he had just been elected minister in charge of literacy, he himself was illiterate.

She tilted her head and thought. "So," she said, "there's some hope?"

"What do you mean?"

"Marcel may hang himself?"

I laughed. "Marcel's your supervisor?"

"Yes. But like I said, he's too busy shopping or smoking hashish. Or boffing his new girl."

Her tone of voice was an unsuccessful attempt at emotional detachment. Marcel's previous girlfriend was herself.

"I never introduced myself," I said, and I used my real name.

"Aurélie Hardouin," she said and we shook hands over the table quite formally. But she was thinking of something else. "Did that story actually happen?" she asked.

"Sure it happened. You heard it."

"No. I mean, did the incidents in it actually take place?"

"Was the curtain rope actually velvet?"

"The main facts."

"Oh. *Facts.* Difficult to say."

A stab of pain across her eyes. "But is it the *truth*?" She said, pouting, looking for some ledge to hang onto, one solid thing in a sea around her. She looked vulnerable and lovely. Women to whom you are attracted have all the power. You will tell them things you wouldn't tell your brother. You want to impress them. "The truth," I said, "is not the storyteller's concern."

"Very convenient," she said. "Where'd you hear that story you just told me?"

"The guy from Tours? I made it up."

"Really?"

"Yes."

"Just then? On the spot?"

"Yep."

"So. You admit that you're a liar?"

"A storyteller."

She considered the difference. "How's that done?" she said.

"Telling a story?"

"Yes."

I glimpsed the Muse out of the corner of my eye. "I'll show you," I said. "For instance: How'd you get this job of yours?"

"What? Oh. I don't quite know, to be honest. I was studying anthropology ..."

"*She* was studying anthropology," I said.

"Sorry?"

"I can never tell a story if I'm too close."

"Oh. OK," she said. "She was studying anthropology, and I ... *she*, heard that they wanted somebody to help out in the Department of Folklore. Then ... well, it got complicated ..."

"How about this?" I said. "*Once upon a time there was a girl who liked to see how people behaved. At family gatherings she used to sit in the corner and watch how her uncle would argue with her father, how her mother would talk to her sister-in-law and she used to imagine that they were a primitive tribe on an island, and not a family in a small village in France."*

"Yes. Well, not exactly ..."

"Well it's a story, you know. Not judicial testimony."

"In that case." She looked up for a second and the ghost of a smile flickered across her lips. Maybe she had glimpsed her Muse as well. *"Then she read a book about a woman who went to live with a primitive tribe, and she thought she would like to do that, so she read other books and discovered that there were jobs to be had and studies to be followed which would make that possible. So when the time came to leave school she enrolled in University and took the courses which would help her go to foreign lands to study the people there. But she was told that there were many others who wanted to do that as well, and that she would have to have patience, establish some solid groundwork and continue to do the things deemed necessary by people above her before she even thought of flying off somewhere. So she hit the books and passed her exams and wrote papers and collated field-work which other people had collected. But in the little cubicle in the basement which was her "office" she had pictures on the wall of the places she'd love to go: Zanzibar, Thule, Terra del Fuego, Bylot Island and Marrakech."*

"Good one," I said.

"Thank you. At any rate: *One day, into her office, strode a man named Marcel."*

"Maurice."

"OK. Maurice ...," she said, then she stopped. She looked at the corner of the tablecloth for quite a long time, absolutely motionless.

"Maybe if you just answer yes or no," I said. "He was an awful person?"

"No."

"Let's say *weak*."

"Oh yes, he was weak."

"And she was ... not stupid, certainly ... but *naïve*, maybe?"

"Not even that."

"Innocent?"

"Yes. That's better."

I picked up her thread and suggested: *"And she would never, in her innocence, have believed he would have behaved in the way he later did."*

"Yes."

"OK. And he was, what? From a neighbouring department?"

"Yes," she said, primed again. *"And he was quite attractive ..."*

"Wouldn't it be better, for the sake of the story," I said, "to make him ugly?" But she ignored me.

"... With blue eyes."

"Squinty, bloodshot and dirt coloured," I said.

"And he had a certain charm about him."

"He was a miserable little evil man, manipulative and dishonest."

"But she didn't know that."

"Because she was kind and innocent?"

"Exactly."

"And extremely beautiful."

"Thank you."

"You're welcome. But it's not about you ..." I was about to say: "Not that you're not beautiful," but she was back into her story now.

"And as it turns out, it was her beauty and innocence, and not her good, solid work which attracted him."

"The rat."

"Well. The truth is he started to fool himself. (OK. The story. I know.) *He felt ... younger in her presence and he took to coming by every afternoon.*"

"This ugly man with warts on his face who smelled so badly?"

"He told her that she was doing some work which seemed interesting, and asked her if she would like to get involved with a study he was conducting on the Arabic storytelling tradition."

"Lying through his rotten teeth."

"So naturally I said yes."

"Naturally she said yes, not realizing that in his basement he had twelve other women chained up, enticed in exactly the same way."

"Well, no ..."

"Nice thought, though."

"How is that a nice thought?"

"I mean, it would be nice if you felt the need to tell the story like that. It would show that you treated him with the contempt he obviously deserves."

"Oh."

We both fell silent, which I broke by saying: "But there was another girl?"

"Yes. It seems that ... Maurice, was it?"

"Yes, Maurice Bluebeard."

"Stop it. *It seems that once a year Maurice used to go on a field trip.*"

"I know what's next," I said. *"And once a year he hired a new 'field assistant'?"*

"In a nutshell ...," she said, frowning quickly.

"And this was looked upon with suspicion by the people who worked with him, and who knew what was going on. But since his work was turned in on time, in a manner which was not completely embarrassing to the department, and because he

had tenure, they considered that they should treat his work as professionals, and not pass judgment on his private life at all."

"But this beautiful, innocent girl ..."

"... thought that when he had her loaned to his department for field study, on the basis of her work, it was just that."

"And not the snivelling machinations of a toad-like troll who exploited innocence and then, once he'd used them for his own vile purposes, discarded them like so much soiled laundry."

"Wait now," she said. "For one thing, I at least partly suspected what his interest in me was."

"But she thought she could somehow steer that back into getting some work done, work which was in fact quite good, coming as it did from a clean place, unpolluted by other desires or devices than to do the job and only the job, simply and well."

"Well, yes."

"You can say that, you see, when it's not about you."

"Right. *She figured if she could just spurn his advances, and just do the work, she would be able to present some incontestably good studies to the department. Not knowing that the department had long since lost all notion of what good work was. So compromised were they with having to deal with Maurice Bluebeard, in whom she had no real interest, outside of what access he could provide."* She stopped. "Yes," she said, "I see how it's done. But. It wasn't as cut and dried as that."

"No. That was just how she thought about it later."

"The only way she could have thought about it later. To give herself the self-esteem necessary to continue with the one thing that mattered to her, and what should have mattered to her."

"Yes. More or less."

"What really happened?" I asked. She looked up.

"Well, I *was* attracted, a little."

"Oh."

"Sure. Why not?"

"What about the drooling and nose-picking?" I said.

"*She overlooked them. She found herself thinking what was the harm if she did have an affair with him? Maybe this was what it was like being grown up.*"

"*He confused her with his evil little lies.*"

"*As he fooled himself.*"

"*Which he found convenient to do, the better to control the selfish little world he had built around him.*"

"But as I say, it wasn't as cut and dried as all that," said Aurélie.

"*And still afterwards, she would defend him, as a lost soul, and not the evil dwarf with snotty lips who made her life a polluted confusion. Even though she knew that the problem was not the world, but his presence in it ...*"

She picked up the thread. "*As there likely would be other people in it like him.*"

"Not as bad *as* him, though."

"OK. For the sake of the story, let's say he's the worst person ever."

"Let's. And that became clear to her when?"

"When he announced that another girl would be coming along on the junket."

"Which of course he didn't say anything about until the last moment when our heroine couldn't do anything about it?"

"*And had already bought both tickets. So there was nothing she could do but tag along and do all the grunt work that had to be done to justify the junket, work which they could take home and take credit for. And meanwhile all the time she had to watch herself being replaced by this new woman, who had moved into the very room which our heroine had even booked.*"

"And that's it?"

"No."

"So, what else?"

"Then she found out something really lousy."

"What?"

"That he was planning to get her removed from his department."

"Why?"

"He was worried that she would file a sexual harassment suit against him."

"And would she?"

"No. Though knowing he could stoop that low, get her removed, he would certainly deserve it."

"That *is* low of him."

"Oh Yes. Well. He's frightened. And in trouble."

"So how did she get even?"

"Even?"

"Yes. How does she break the chains, pick the lock, overcome the guard, and escape the dungeon he has locked her in?"

"Oh. The best part."

"Yes."

"I don't know. But it was driving her insane."

"May I make a suggestion?"

"Sure."

"*Well, there came one day a white knight in shining armour, handsome and good ...*"

"Oh boy."

"*... And seeing a lady in distress, and having made a vow to aid all such fair ladies, he swore to help her.*"

"Bravo. He must've been an incredible man."

"*Without fear and without reproach. He drew his sword and slew the ogre, first mutilating him horribly, although the result turned out to be actually an improvement.*"

"No. It didn't quite happen like that ..."

"*This brave knight then sent him to hell where he burnt for eternity.*"

"Not exactly."

"What then?"

"This brave knight then talked to her," she said.

"Doesn't seem very knight-like. Strong and silent, but excellent with a broadsword, I would have said."

"Certainly not silent. You could barely shut him up. Which was alright. He was a good talker, though he tended to speak in riddles and poems."

"But he liked to think that they were healing riddles, though. The type which help. He was a man of mystery, perhaps?"

"A certain amount, yes."

"Which only increased her attraction for him. But he didn't act that way just to be mysterious. He acted that way for the right reasons."

"Which are?"

"Love, of course." There. I'd said it. But I had said the word like it was a philosophical principle, not an emotion.

She paused for a while. "Yes," she said. "That's the difference."

"Yes."

"She got the sense that although he was tricky, this brave knight, he was basically a good man."

"And devilishly handsome."

"And very conceited."

"Well played! So what did he do?" I was the audience now.

"Well, there was none of this cleaving of chains with his mighty broadsword."

"Too bad. Much more dramatic."

"But not as real."

"Hmm."

"He took a link of the chain and looked at it, and understood it, and got it to tell its story. And as he did, the chains,

forged in the hottest hate of hell, from iron became lead, then pewter, and finally foam, which melted and fell off, and she was free."

I was impressed. "Well told," I said. "So *then* he commanded her to slay the ogre with a mighty blow?"

"No. Worse."

"What then?"

She thought about it for a bit. "She ... forgot about him."

"Interesting. Didn't send him to hell?"

"Nope. Left him in hell where he already was."

"Bravo," I said.

"Thanks," she said, then added: "I'm not trying to forgive him, though."

I thought of the cop and the community, the falcon and the dove and the fear, and it occurred to me that maybe at the root that this was the same. "There are worse things," I said.

"Yes yes," she said impatiently. "And I'll forgive, eventually. Sometime. Later. Much later. Unless I don't." She shuddered, then picked up the thread. "But I'm saying I'm not trying to forgive him now. Just understand him, so I can avoid turning out *like* him."

The waiter arrived, and she took the bill.

"Easy for me not to get emotional about it," I said. "I'm not involved."

"Am I boring you with my problems?"

"Not at all. It's what friends are for."

"We're friends?"

"Sure."

"That's nice."

"Yes."

We didn't say anything for a little while. Time to go. "Well, thank you very much," I said. "Would you like me to walk you to your hotel?"

"Yes. We're finished here."

We walked down to street level and made our way across the Djemma to where Boulevard Mohammad Cinq arrives at the Koutoubia. There were probably shorter ways to get back to her hotel, but they meant going by smaller more confusing streets. On the way I told her a story about how I got lost in the souks for six hours one day, and was starting to panic, when I remembered how all the mosques faced Mecca and I used them to orient myself out. It wasn't a bad story, and had never happened though it wasn't really a lie, because I only wanted to entertain her. I was concentrating on what I was saying, and it came as a shock when we arrived at the hotel. It was the same hotel I had escaped from that morning just ahead of being kicked out.

I stopped. There was somebody in the doorman's booth now.

"All right," I said. "I'll leave you here."

"Oh," she said, and, darling girl, she looked disappointed. She said she hoped she would see me at the Djemma next day. I said that would be nice and kissed her chastely on both cheeks.

She said goodbye, then, just as I was turning away, said: "Wait."

"Yes?"

"If you want, I could hire you to translate those other stories I collected."

"O ... K ...," I said.

"You hesitate."

"It's just, well, I'd have to listen to them from the tape."

"Take the tape recorder with you." Then while I hesitated again she made it worse. "Don't worry," she said. "I trust you."

"When should we meet?" I asked her, and she gave me a time and place. I said goodbye again, took my leave and started back to the Djemma. Such sweet sorrow.

As I walked back, the tape recorder bumped alongside my hip, but it wasn't heavy at all. Although I wasn't worth her trust yet, I could make it right.

Back at the Djemma the widow was just packing up. The guy who was in charge of her business was looking at me, wondering if he should approach.

"Asalaam Alaykam," I said.

"Wa'Alaykam Asalaam," said he, smiling that remarkable smile which changed his face completely, and he started speaking rapidly in Arabic.

"I don't speak Arabic," I said.

"Oh," he said. Then an "Oh," of realization, and a third "Oh," this time impressed.

"Yes," I said. "But there are some stories I have here on tape to translate. Could you help me out?"

"I would be honoured," he said. He actually said that.

"Earlier tonight was special," I explained. "For these?" I tapped the recorder. "How much?"

"How many stories?"

"Three. No. Four. I don't have *much* money now."

"Ah," he said sympathetically, sad for me, not himself. "Well, you overpaid me last time. You tell *me* how much."

All in all a much more civilized way of doing business. "She gave me two hundred," I said. "I'll take half and give you half, same as before. Tomorrow you can listen and translate, I'll transcribe. But I'll need some money for food and for a room to sleep, say fifty. That's a hundred and fifty, half and half. How does seventy-five euros sound?"

"You can sleep at my house," he said. "My wife will cook you food. She is an artist in the kitchen. Save your money, then give us half of the two hundred."

"Much better," I said.

"Much better," he agreed, and we shook hands.

"I'll need paper," I said.

"No problem," he said.

His name was Nuradeen, and he lived East of the souks in an atypical ryad, with his family, two girls and one boy, as well as his wife and the widow. I never did quite catch how she was related to him. We came in through the small courtyard and I was introduced and welcomed. His wife went to prepare mint tea, and after he talked with me for a while he left me alone for a minute, I suppose to explain to her what I was doing here. He came back, we talked some more and, when she reappeared, it was with tea and pastries, gazelle horns, and a delicious honey confection. The children were asleep and we kept our voices to a low murmur.

We finished and he showed me to my room, which his wife had made up, and I washed in a basin full of warm water on a sideboard. I arranged my things, and folded my shirt and put it under the mattress to press it. I laid out my possessions from my satchel, then put them back in order. By rearranging the contents I could now fit even the recorder inside. It really was a miraculous satchel. I washed my socks and bathing suit, rung them out and laid them on the windowsill where the morning sun would dry them. I lay down on the bed and as I closed my eyes I immediately remembered everything I had thought about the night before, and it all seemed possible again. My shoulders were tired, I realized, from standing straighter than I usually do, in Aurélie's presence. Love improves you.

Like taking my possessions out and laying them side by side, I took out my actions of the last two days. I had no problem with what I had done at the party in the ryad in Essaouira, nor with the use of the pool at Aurélie's hotel. The people at the party in the ryad had been entertained for their food and wine, and at the hotel I had paid for the coffee, which was grossly overpriced. On the bus ride in, the clients got a running commentary (complete with the goat story) which, while probably not terrifically factual, was at least diverting, and in my estimation, that had more than paid for at least my journey. The tips were their choice, freely given, gratefully received, and I had shared them with the driver.

But what about the other tour guide? The one I had tricked into staying in Essaouira? Would he lose his job? I wouldn't want that, and I considered ways that I could prevent it from happening.

Then there was Aurélie. If someone who knew Arabic heard the tape, then read her transcription of my "translation," she could get into trouble. Short of coming clean, I'm not sure what I could do about that. I may have to follow her back to France to set things right. I laughed at the idea but then thought: What the hell else do I have to do that's as important as that? It was like I was going a bit mad. But there was magic in my life now.

I fell asleep and slept like a log. There is absolutely nothing like feeling good about yourself. I would make everything right.

And that of course was when everything started to go wrong.

WOKE UP next morning, fell asleep again for an hour, and woke and rose when I heard noises outside the room. I washed, shaved, checked that I had everything and went downstairs.

"Good morning," said Nuradeen and we asked each other how we had slept. Wife, widow and children were there. He said something sharp in Arabic to his children, which I suppose meant to stop staring, because they did. He introduced everybody formally to me, and we ate croissants and oranges and drank coffee. I complimented Nuradeen's wife on the meal and then the children were sent off to school. The little boy looked at me and, just before he ran off, stuck his tongue out at me, the little brat. I had to laugh.

Nuradeen had some business to do, and so did I, and I mentioned again that I would need some paper. He translated this to his wife, she fetched two school note-books and I thanked them both. Then Nuradeen had to leave, and I said I had to go as well, as I should write some things down. If I wanted, offered Nuradeen, I could do that here, but I thought that he may be uncomfortable leaving me alone with the widow and his wife, so I declined the offer. He didn't actually show his relief, but you could see that he thought that that would perhaps be best. We both left at the same time, agreeing to meet in a few hours back here. He went one way and I went the other. I found a café around a corner, ordered tea, took the previous day's writing out of my satchel, reread it, and started in on what followed. I found that if I concentrated on writing legibly, in fast straight lines, the words came naturally and the events unfolded in their own steady rhythm. I worked quite happily until I had written myself back to this café, and it was now time to go meet Nuradeen.

We sat in his courtyard and I cued the recorder to the stories that Aurélie had collected, gave him the earphones and pressed play. "Ah," he said. "Ibraim ...," recognizing the storyteller with a small snort of contempt. He listened, pushed pause, translated out loud, and continued as I transcribed.

"Not a very good one," he said when it finished. "Ah well, Ibraim does his best."

The widow showed up for the third story, but didn't say anything, and then I cued the recorder to the story I had created from her rhythms which I had written down from memory that morning at the cafe.

You could hear both our voices, hers in the background, but Nuradeen knew the story well and so had no problem relating what she said to me. It turns out that it was about two young boys and a fig garden. The widow listened in and Nuradeen explained to her what we were doing. She pointed to herself questioningly, and listened more closely: she hadn't recognized her own voice. Then she said something to Nuradeen who translated for me that she thought that it would make a story, how a lady heard her own story in her own voice, didn't recognize it, and accused another lady of stealing her stories. I told her, through Nuradeen, that I too thought that would make a good story. I pushed "play" and, while I transcribed what Nuradeen told me, Nuradeen translated for her what I was saying on the tape. As I transcribed, I could see her becoming more curious about my story. She was taking a professional interest, in some places even nodding approval. In this way we continued until both our stories came to an end. She nodded again, said something to me, and touched Nuradeen on the shoulder to get him to translate.

"She says that your story is better than hers," said Nuradeen.

"I would be honoured if you told it," I said to her. Nuradeen translated this to her. "But I have a better one," I said, and I started to tell her the story of the goat in the tree, with Nuradeen translating as well. When I finished she smiled and stood up, thanking me, and thinking about how she would tell it on the Djemma that night, deciding what she could add or edit. I saw her leaving, thinking about it, an artist mulling over a new lump of material to shape.

"I think we've got everything," I said. And then the children came back from school. The two girls said hello politely and then went to see their mother, and the boy decided to stay with us. He seemed impatient and asked his father the time twice. "There's a show on television he likes," said Nuradeen.

"Do you know the one about the boy who watched so much television he fell through the screen?" I asked him.

"No," he said.

So I made one up for him until it was time. He was a bit distracted at first while it sounded like it was going to have a moral, but I got his attention, as you get the attention of young boys, with action and victory. Revenge works too. With girls, tales of trust, betrayal and the power of attraction are what's called for. I have no idea what this signifies: it's only what I have observed.

When I finished, Nuradeen said: "Your show is on. Be careful that you don't fall through the screen." And his boy ran off. Nuradeen said he was going to the mosque and I said I had to be leaving. "Stay for supper," he offered, but I said that I had to meet somebody.

"The girl?" he asked.

I said: "Yes."

"She is beautiful," he said.

"Yes," I said.

And now, I thought, I have to make myself worthy of her. I felt good and noble as I said goodbye to Nuradeen and walked toward my rendezvous, but that was an hour and a half away, so I took a seat in another café where the covering on the table was a sheet of blank newsprint. I asked if I could have it after I had ordered tea, the waiter said fine, so I removed it from the table and folded it into four, creased it carefully into notepaper size, then tore it neatly along the crease and wrote on one sheet: "This note is to inform whom it may concern that I am the man who fooled your tour guide into staying in Essaouira so that I could take his place and get a free ride to Marrakech. I would not like him to receive any blame for this. I also duped your driver, and the passengers, your customers. Please accept my sincerest apologies, as well as your advertised fare which you should find enclosed."

Taking the remainder of the sheet, I folded it in three and, using it as a template, measured the other quarto of the newsprint for the envelope. Some glue would have been handy, but it was not really a problem as I once studied with an origami master in Kyoto. (Not really. I've never been to Japan.)

I folded the corners into each other, thought about it, couldn't get it to hold on its own, then saw how I should have started. After three tries I figured out how to make an envelope, but it was creased awkwardly with the previous attempts, so setting aside that piece to use as writing paper tomorrow, I started again.

It's like the paper-folder of Japan, I told myself. *His name was Boku and all day he folded here, folded there, until he had an envelope ...* I started on my envelope, and told myself the story.

He made them twelve to a package, which he placed in a flat box of folded paper he also made. He was very good at what he did, and demand was high and so his fame spread across the country. Everybody asked: Who is this man who makes these marvellous envelopes? They sent words of praise to him to which he would respond by sending back an empty envelope, but of such pleasing dimensions and with creases so artistic that they understood: that was his answer; thank you for asking. The Emperor himself sent him a note and he sent back an envelope with a representation of a crane folded into the back, every feather of its outstretched wing creased into its surface, and the wind ruffling his neck feathers, so finely done that if you looked at it you could not help but shiver to feel the wind on your own neck.

There were some merchants in the neighbouring village who heard about him, and heard what people said about his envelopes, and saw how people who owned them valued them. They tried to buy some, but nobody would sell them any, and then they knew they had to have them. It made them feel that there was some value outside money, which disturbed them, and made them a little frightened.

So they went to see the paper-folder. "We will give you money," they said, and he said:

"The baker comes by, leaves me the bread, and takes an envelope. The tea-grower comes by and leaves me tea and does the same. The boy who catches fish off the wharf delivers them fresh and takes an envelope. The paper-maker gives me more

paper to fold in exchange for folded paper. Please do me the honour of taking an envelope before you go."

The merchants said thank you, then each took an envelope and left. Once they were home they pooled the envelopes, took what they considered was the best example and had it carefully unfolded, making notes on how to refold it. Then they hired the deftest person in the village to reconstruct it, but when the reconstruction was finished, although all the steps were reproduced exactly, the end result was not quite the same. Something wasn't right. The merchants nevertheless started manufacturing their copies, but now people started talking about "an original Boku," and people who owned these originals were deemed people of great taste and foresight. So, although the merchants sold a few envelopes, the value of theirs didn't rise, and their reputation went downhill, which made them even more desperate. Now they hired scholars from the university to study Boku. They observed him, then wrote monographs and articles on his supposed method and seeing so much funding arrive for studies about Boku, the scholars formed a faculty of envelope-folding studies under the umbrella of a paper-folding wing at the university, and held conferences in neighbouring universities, and now they didn't even need Boku, the endless chess-game of intramural politics engaging them much more than this business of folding paper, which was rather unimportant, when you thought about it.

But eventually the merchants started to demand results, whispering to each other that the scholars were perhaps not that wise after all. Fear crept into the university, hints of other peoples' errors were made by colleagues, grudges were nourished, and meanwhile Boku kept folding his envelopes.

Finally, from the university one professor was elected to try talking to him again and by this time they were all quite angry with Boku. The professor started graciously, set out humbly the difficulties they were having with the situation, but was met only with passive compassion from Boku. Eventually, frustrated, the professor's argument devolved into: "Well, aren't you selfish! If you don't tell us how you do it, we will stop studying you."

"Here," said Boku. "Please accept from me an envelope." Then the professor, softening as he looked at it, then hardening himself to the good feelings which welled up inside him which would make it impossible for him to do his duty. "You are not alone in this world!" snapped the professor. "And politically, you are naive!"

Boku bowed humbly. "I am indeed honoured."

The professor went back to the university and conferred with some other academics. The merchants who were funding the project were now openly threatening that if they didn't get that secret soon they would close down the department, and they held a massive all-faculty meeting.

By this time the paper-folder was branching out and making other things besides envelopes and the boxes he placed them in: wild animals, dragons, and curious figures of all sorts. He had reached a level with his art that he would start with a piece of paper, then fold here, fold there, regard the result which suggested something, and by folding in a corner here, back-folding this and hiding the corner in a crease there, he could make a recognizable shape. "What is it?" said the children who gathered around after school to watch him work, and then, when it appeared: "Oh, it's a pelican!" Or a monkey, or a toad playing a lute. One day the children arrived and there were a series of folded paper tubes, one for each child. "What are they?" said the children. "Are your lips dry?" asked the paper-folder. "Yes? Then each of you take one and blow into it." And the children did. "They're whistles!" they said, and ran out into the village causing people to complain about the sound.

"Uh-oh," said the paper folder, as he went back to folding paper and, when the children came back in a few days, having worn out all their whistles or blown them with wet lips and thereby ruining them, or having fought over them and ripped them (as is normal for children to do), there was a new set waiting for them, tuned to lovely low notes which harmonized with each other and which nobody complained about, and which in fact inspired the teacher in the village to start up a music class where they eventually featured in a performance.

Meanwhile the professor was putting the economy of the University on a war-time footing, concocting schemes by which they could surround the paper-folder and force him to submit to their will. They had to get control of this increasingly potent force in the village. When they heard people talk about this miraculous paper-folder, they publicly agreed but privately thought harder about how to dominate him. They formed a coalition with the merchants who submitted their problem to the Government who agreed with them that this man was a threat to the established order. But what could the Government do?

"Send in troops and take all known examples of his art as being important parts of the National Heritage which should be protected," suggested the representative of the coalition. "Then impose restrictions on whomever he distributes to."

But the Government considered that this would be too extreme and counter-productive.

"So you're saying," said the representative, "that the Government, the all-mighty rulers of this great land, can do nothing?"

"No," said a Government official. "I'm saying that, if we do, we'll have to be sneaky." And the professors and the merchants smiled, because they were quite comfortable with the idea of sneakiness. In fact, as folding paper was the paper-folder's art, being sneaky was theirs.

They followed the baker who supplied the paper-folder with bread and closed him down because of the unhealthy method he used and which they had just dreamed up, but

other bakers supplied the paper-folder with bread in ex-
change for his work. So they followed the boy who brought him
fish, and shut him down for not having a new license which
they had initiated for the purpose. But other fishermen sup-
plied him, and the professors and Government officials and
merchants conferred again. "He isn't shut down yet, but his
supply lines are getting thin, even though his work is becoming
increasingly more impressive. I saw a frog which not only
jumped but, if you pushed its back, its neck swelled up and,
from inside where a flap of paper rubbed against a serrated
piece, it emitted a croak. Genius!"

"Have you seen the hedgehog playing an accordion, which
when you set it down on the table will actually play a real
tune?"

"The weight depresses a set of bellows which expels air
through whistles," said another.

"We are not here to sing the praises of this miserable paper-
folder!" snapped the professor who, by this time with the
weight of power he had being conferred with, experienced
wrenching pains in his belly, and talked with a little line of
spittle around his lips. "There is no doubt that he is talented.
But he is endangering the very system which protects him and
allows him to continue to create. We have to stop him. People
are starting to say that there's a conspiracy against him, and
suspecting us. Now, if we cannot stop the paper-folder by cut-
ting off his supply of food, I suggest we cut off his supply of
paper".

And so they burnt down the paper factory ...

Here it looked like my envelope was finishing up now,
almost on its own. One more tuck and I would have it.

But the paper-folder folded up a new paper factory out of huge
sheets of paper.

I creased over a very small sharp corner.

And the Government burnt it down as well.

I saw where I could insert the corner to finish it up neatly.

So he built another better one. And they burnt that one down too. And the paper-folder and the politicians kept at it, the paper-folder creating, the politicians destroying, all their lives until they were old men. And then they all died.

But the paper-folder died happy, and the politicians did not.

I looked at the envelope. Pathetically perhaps, I was rather proud of the results, then thought that maybe it was not so pathetic. Like writing, all I was doing was adding value to blank paper. And as an art, origami wasn't bad. Like storytelling, the most important moment was the next one, built on the moment before, and figuring how paper could be folded in a certain way, creasing it exactly and ending up with a satisfying functional shape, maybe that was something that you could actually do which added to the sum of good things in the world. At the very least I now thought that was possible, which was certainly better than that awful pointlessness I had felt last winter in Essaouira, with the wind howling above my roof, and me lying in bed, almost not able to move. At that time I would not have seen the point of folding paper into anything.

So I had got this far, and if I wanted to get further I would have to take the next step. I paid, left the café and walked through the Djemma to the Koutoubia, back up Mohammed Cinq through the Bab and up to the travel bureau where I had arrived from Essaouira. What it was going to take now was humility.

The driver I wanted to see was standing outside his bus. I approached him, he recognized me and I saw his face fall, wondering whether I had become a problem, wanting to sleep in his baggage compartment again, an entanglement because of an act of kindness on his part. He said hello warily.

"I've come to pay my fare," I said, and he loosened and smiled. I wouldn't be a burden.

"How have you been?" he said.

"Good," I said. "I was worried that the other tour guide might get in trouble."

He dropped his voice and looked back at the office. "Aziz? No. I covered for him."

"Good."

"I told them in the office that I would meet him around the corner the next morning, and then I picked up my nephew. He drove and I told them your story on the way down."

"How did they like it?" I asked.

"Good. Do you mind that I stole it from you?"

"I stole a ride from the company," I said, and I gestured with the envelope.

"What's this?"

"My fare."

"Keep your money," he said grandly. "I think maybe from now on Aziz will be driving, and I will be doing the talking."

"Well, at least take half," I said. "For the place to sleep." He protested but relented and then thanked me. We shook hands.

A blessing, I thought as I walked back, and 15 euros extra as well. If this was the way making amends worked, I should have started earlier. I felt light of heart and could think without pain of what had happened in Paris, wondering if I was the one who had been weak or devious there, but deciding that what occurred could not have happened any other way.

The first time I had felt that confusion, it was behind my brow in front of my brain, hard to identify where exactly, since it was partly what did the identifying. But while telling stories, I had stumbled, or had to force things into shape and, when I went to that place to fill out the picture I was describing, it was tender as a bruise. It was a bit frightening, to tell the truth, but I found myself still having another story due. How was it that I had another story due? What set of agreements had made it so that I was expected to show up and come up with a story at a certain time? How could those stories bear anything but the aspect of the prison I was in? Cold, geometric, functional, serving only to build a wall around any talents I might have?

Now though, on the Boulevard Mohammed Cinq, I was glad I had left. The desert had bloomed again, and that dull tender bruise behind my forehead was clear and fearless. It was doing its job, and its job now on this day of rebirth was to somehow help this girl I had lied to. Our fates were inextricably entwined. She was a damsel in distress. I was her knight in shining armour, without fear and without reproach.

I walked back to the Djemma as the sun went down over the souks and the tintinnabulation was starting. I wandered from crowd to crowd, not stopping long enough to be obliged to pay. I went to the cafe where we said we would meet, sat down and ordered mint tea. I fiddled with the tape recorder for a bit and worked out how to erase the story I had told her on the Djemma the night before. I debated to myself whether I really should, then decided. There was something very final about pushing that button to delete.

Then, like in a poorly constructed novel where characters arrive exactly when the action demands it, I saw my love come through the door and up to the table.

"You made it," she said.

"At the very least I had to give you back your recorder," I said. "I had a problem with it, though, so I have some bad news."

"Oh no. What?"

"Somehow I managed to erase that first story I translated." I handed her the notebooks with the real translations. "Here. I transcribed it for you, but I pushed some button somewhere on your machine and damned if I can find the original recording now." Very soon I would have to stop this, but taking off your armour is scary.

"Oh well. Too bad," she said, not terrifically disturbed. She opened the notebook I handed her. "Nice penmanship."

"It's something I pride myself on," I said, then thought: see how simple it was to just tell the truth?

"Now," she said, "I would like to treat you to dinner." And that was my reward.

"It's expensive here on the Djemma," I said. "I know a cheaper place."

"I like the view here," she said.

"Where *do* you get the money?" I asked.

"It's a junket," she said and rolled her eyes. That little line between her eyebrows creased. I recognized that she herself was starting to feel that fuzzy spot behind her brow. "They give you a per diem which you have to spend, then a budget which if you don't spend will reduce the money they give you next year and some other department will take it over. So the pressure is on you to waste money. But it's not the money. God, it would be easy if it was just *money*." A statement which ran contrary to my experience.

"What is it then?"

"The false position. The politics. The compromises. The hidden agendas. The egos. The bullying. The lies."

So it was probably not a good time to spring on her that I had lied to her.

Although, I told myself, they're not really lies. They're stories. If I was going to talk a suicide down from a ledge, and I heard on the way there that his cat had died, would I tell him that, or would I keep that from him? And if I did would I be lying? ... But those were *my* problems. What she needed was something that would help her.

"I heard another one today ...," I started.

There once lived a Young Man east of here who owned two donkeys, and because people from his village kept saying what lovely donkeys they were, he grew proud of them, and groomed them when they sweated, and kept their hooves clean and dry. One of them was a good and handsome donkey and the other was not so good, but he loved them equally and treated them both the same, and treated them well.

I thought of taking it to where somebody came with three donkeys, and him thinking, "How lovely it would be to have three," but to have the story play out that way was not relevant to her predicament or pain.

One day a Donkey Trader arrived and said: "I see you have two donkeys."

"Yes," said the Young Man, who was by now quite used to people congratulating him on them, and who in fact enjoyed it when they did. "Aren't they lovely?"

But the Donkey Trader said: "I don't know about 'lovely.' The best one is splay-footed and hammer-headed, and the worst is swaybacked, pigeon-chested, wall-eyed, bow-legged, knock-kneed, and croupy.'

The Young Man was shocked. He had never heard such rudeness before and he wished to correct the man, but more than that, he wished he could demand an apology.

"You are wrong about that," said the Young Man, coldly, and the Donkey Trader laughed contemptuously.

"Anyone who would own such donkeys is probably blind to their faults," he said, and walked away.

The rest of the day the Young Man was angry. He went about his business under a dark cloud, with his brow scowled down as he fed his donkeys and tossed straw bedding under them, and his donkeys thought: What's wrong with the Young Man? He hasn't brushed my coat although we are sweating, and the water trough is empty although we are thirsty.

The next day the Young Man asked around town about that rude Donkey Trader and the people in the village could see that something was poisoning him. He walked around in a funk and carelessly fed and watered his donkeys, who thought: What is wrong with him? He hasn't mucked out the paddock, and still hasn't groomed us, and there are burrs in our manes and tails and our hooves need to be cleaned.

So obsessed was the Young Man with the Donkey Trader's comments, so distracted with the idea that someone would say such things, that he started to ignore his charges. Right now the Donkey Trader was probably telling everybody how he had seen two of the worst donkeys he had ever seen, and the thought of these people laughing at how the Donkey Trader described them distracted him further. Sway-backed! (And he absently slapped his prize donkey on the back, on a sore which had developed). That is the straightest back in the region! And I'm sure that that Donkey Trader's donkeys were twice as swaybacked as these. How could he say such things?

Thoughts like this, unless they are kept in check with prayer and gratitude, spread slowly, consuming like smouldering wood. And so it was that, when he went about his work cutting hay, his neighbours could see him stop, put down his scythe, then stand back and talk to the field, moving his hands in agitation, because in his mind he was talking to the Donkey Trader. And meanwhile his donkeys had developed a cough.

The next day the Donkey Trader showed up again, and looked at the prize donkey and said: "He has a cold." And although the Young Man had in fact heard the cough, such was the enmity he had nursed that he refused to admit it, even to himself. The Donkey Trader could not be right. His donkey coughed again. "There," said the Donkey Trader, and the word cut the man like a knife. "Donkey Trader," he said, "you would not know a cold from a simple cough." And then the Donkey Trader walked away contemptuously. The man was incensed. He started to yell something after the Donkey Trader, but then his donkey coughed again. And the man turned and said: "Why did you have to cough?" And all the bottled up anger he had for the Donkey Trader he took out on his donkey. "You deserve to have a cough! And so that you know, stupid donkey, that I am angry with you, and to teach you obedience, I will only feed you half your ration tonight, and you can go without grooming." And his donkey looked back at him thinking: Why is he like this? And the man stomped out and blocked his ears to the coughs of his donkey in the stall. And the next morning he woke up and his donkey was dead, and when he saw him lying in the paddock, not breathing, still as stone, he realized his foolishness and wept, and the Donkey Trader, who heard about it, laughed, for the Donkey Trader was the Devil.

"How sad," said the girl.

"Yes. A cautionary tale."

"It's true," she said. "They get you so wound up you can't think of the job at hand."

I could see her taking the story into herself, and that tender spot behind her forehead started to what? Harden? No, but, flower, or get greener, sprout. Her shoulders relaxed.

"Tea?" she offered.

Now, take this very slowly, I thought. I'll be a lodestar for you, who is a lodestar for me. Am I fooling myself? Possibly. Am I fooling her? Unforgiveable.

I poured tea, the sun went down, as fuzzy around the edges as that place behind the forehead. We looked out across the roofs with the satellite dishes and the minarets. The city and the Koutoubia glowed like sunburnt flesh. We talked. I paid.

"Ouch," I said. "That mint must have been grown in gold dust and crushed emeralds."

She laughed. We stood up and the waiter smiled at us like we were a couple. We walked downstairs and outside and then we bought a watermelon in a large basement market opening onto the Djemma. I carried it on top of my miraculous satchel, its weight supported by the strap. The noise of the Djemma meant that we had to walk closer together to be heard, but even when we came out on the Boulevard we stayed that way.

"The thing is," she said, "if I don't get this work done, I'll probably be out of a job."

"And he's not helping any?"

"No" she said, quite neutrally.

I thought that it was quite true that the way to get out of your own problems was to help somebody else without any hope of advantage to yourself. The fact that I wouldn't mind sleeping with her, the darling, was it seemed to me, honestly quite independent of this desire to help.

"I imagine there are other people in the department who know how he behaves."

"Yes, but they don't seem to be in the position to do anything about it. Or don't want to get so worked up about it that they forget to water the donkey."

"That's the choice."

"But," she said. "If I do the work, he'll just get the credit for it and I'll just be encouraging him."

I waited a bit. "Who's the girl?" I said.

"His assistant," she said. "They deserve each other."

"When are you going back to France?"

"It's open-ended, but I told him that as far as I was concerned it would be sooner rather than later."

"That's OK with him?"

"Oh no. I had to threaten him, and throw a fit." She suddenly laughed at the memory, an ugly cackle, holding her hand over her mouth. She was beautiful.

"You book the flights and hotels?"

"And collect the stories. And organize the events and stop the more absent-minded academics from walking off cliffs. If he could swing it politically, he would probably have me do his laundry as well."

"He is a politician?"

"Oh yes."

"Not like an elected politician though?"

"No no. Not elected. God no. Who'd elect *him*? His main concern is arranging things so that he need never be put to any test like an election. Eliminate any achievement in the process of rising to the top."

"It is a democracy, not a meritocracy."

"From what I've seen it *is* a meritocracy, actually. But the skills which count are political skills, and that's depressing."

"That *is* the way it is," I said, "in *their* world. But you don't have to be like that."

"You do if you want to get on." And she almost seemed pouty. Unattractive. If this kept up I might very well refuse to sleep with her.

We arrived at her hotel. We stopped. "Would you like some watermelon?" she said.

There was nobody in the doorman's booth now and inside the hotel probably there was a different set of employees from the morning shift.

"Certainly," I said.

We walked into the hotel. Nobody I recognized was at the front desk as she picked up her key. I was almost disappointed about that, as I could have established my legitimacy with them now that she was inviting me. We got onto the elevator and rode it up to the fourth floor, walked down the hall to her room, and she had trouble with the key in the lock.

"I'll go get another," she said.

"Let me try," I said, and it actually opened first try, which was a good thing. The sight of a full-grown man swearing and sobbing while pounding and kicking the door might make her reconsider me.

The room was what you'd expect. Pricey, many-chambered and tasteful. Beige and pink, the same colour scheme as the hotel, or indeed, the town. The Rose City, though this colour of paint didn't quite match the patina of the city walls. Through the window you could see flat roofs, TV antennae, the top of a palm tree or two, and a minaret. A crescent moon and Venus hung in the velvet sky. It looked positively phony.

"Package deal," she said.

"How long are you going to be here?"

"Don't know. Should be back in Tours on Tuesday latest. But the tickets are open-ended." As was the statement.

"Watermelon?" I suggested.

"What? Oh, sure." And she went across distractedly and placed the watermelon on a towel and started cutting it.

"Could I use your washroom?" I asked.

"Yes. Sure. In there."

It was bigger than many of the rooms I've lived in, and cleaner and more expensively appointed, too. Individual cotton hand towels in a stack, folded, and a container to throw them in after each washing, where they could be collected, cleaned, scented, and for all I knew re-woven. There was even a phone beside the toilet, which didn't seem right. The sink counter held an array of soaps, shampoos, a sewing kit and a shoehorn all embossed with the logo of the hotel. I pocketed one of the soaps.

By the time I came back into the bedroom, the water-melon was carved and waiting on the coffee table. "Tea?" she asked.

"Certainly," said I, and she filled the pot in the corner and turned it on.

"Camomile, mint, orange pekoe, or Chinese. Oh, and tilleul."

I remembered the new leaves of linden outside the home where I grew up and chose tilleul. She put the bag in the pot and poured the hot water in, then carried it over to the table.

There once was a princess who lived in a palace and, when her father, the King, asked her who she would give her heart to, she said she would give it to whoever could give her a river of diamonds. Her Father thought privately that she should be more concerned with her soul than with jewels, (though actually it was not the jewels themselves that concerned her, but their beauty.) Her father thought about who amongst her acquaintances could afford such a dowry, and lined up two prospects.

"It is traditional to have three suitors," said the Princess, and the father, impatient with her ingratitude said:

"Do you think diamonds lie in the riverbed to be picked up? If that were true then that boy who lives in the hut by the ford would be the richest man in the country!"

"Nevertheless," said the Princess. "Three suitors is the tradition."

Her father sighed, tore some hair out, and to teach her a lesson invited as her third suitor the boy who lived by the ford. "Hey!" he yelled at him out of the window of his carriage, "would you like a shot at marrying my daughter?"

"The princess?" said the boy.

"Who else?" said the King angrily. He was getting more and more frustrated with the whole business.

"Of course," said the boy. "I have long been in love with her from afar."

"Well, good for you," said the King. "Prepare your suit for seven days from now. And, oh yes, if you hope to stand a chance, better bring along a river of diamonds."

And he left, laughing to himself. That would teach his daughter for being so fickle, and teach that upstart of a boy to have the gall to worship his daughter. Young people today!

Early next week, the first suitor came by in a carriage with a retinue, introduced himself, and bowed deeply a rehearsed bow. He was clean shaven, scented and groomed, his nose hairs plucked and the hair on his ears clipped. He wore a tight girdle, and padded stockings to give shape to his legs. He brought the Princess to his palace accompanied by her father, who was mightily impressed. Banners streamed, bells sounded, and when they entered the courtyard a special fanfare of a hundred and twenty-four horns, constructed from brass to play only one note each, arranged on bleachers with their players in a row like the notes of an organ, conducted in a musical composition specially commissioned for her arrival.

"Did you compose that music?" the princess asked the suitor.

"Not 'composed,' no, my lady," said he, "but had the finest composer in the land to honour your presence here and introduce ..." And the orchestra sounded the final chord ... 'A River Of Diamonds!' And a door slid open, and down a velvet-lined trough tumbled diamonds like grain down a chute.

"Not bad," said the Princess. And with that, her father could no longer hold his tongue.

"I'm sure my daughter is so stunned by Your Excellency's efforts that she is speechless with admiration. We will return to our palace now to consider, and will give you our answer when we have seen the other suitor."

"I will give you *my* answer," corrected the Princess, "and only after I have seen the other two suitors."

The King would not talk to his daughter on the way back or that evening at dinner, or for the next three days. He only pulled some more hairs from his head and muttered to himself.

The next day the second suitor arrived, a military man from a castle and foundry which supplied armaments far and wide. He showed up in full armour with a bodyguard of a hundred soldiers, was lowered off his armoured steed by crane, into the middle of his pack of armoured war-dogs, and then marched to the head of his formation outside the walls of the palace and announced: "I have come to marry your daughter."

Just what she needs, thought the King. A strong hand.

He and his daughter were taken by military escort to his castle where they were shown a tournament of war games and jousting, where many bones were broken and there were at least two confirmed kills. Then they were taken on a tour of the foundry, where 120 blacksmiths pounded metal to make the machines which occupied an even bigger space underground, machines which rolled and pounded and thumped and clanged. And in the back of that immense room were giant oak doors which creaked open to reveal an even larger room with one immense machine which geared from a huge wheel on the back wall like a cathedral altar, pressed with immense force on one point, then relaxed with a hiss, as something winked and fell to the ground. And as they walked across the crunchy gravel floor, toward it, they saw that what the machine was doing was pressing diamonds from coal, each of them falling on the ground and spreading across the floor, and that this was the gravel they walked across.

"Behold!" announced the suitor flinging out his armoured arm. "A River Of Diamonds!" And the princess said: "More of a lake, actually."

And the suitor said: "And when they mount to the windows they will flow out in a river, and the river shall flow for as long as I make them!"

And the Princess bent down and picked one up, and straightened and looked at it closely, and said: "So they're not real diamonds, then?"

On the way back her father did not only refuse to talk to her, but occasionally emitted small yelps and pulled his hairs out two and three at a time.

"What was wrong with that one?" he said finally.

"Too stupid," said the Princess.

"You will never marry," said the King when they arrived at their palace. "Two have come and two have been rejected. Nobody is good enough for you!" And he slammed the door.

There are supposed to be three suitors, thought the Princess as she lay in bed.

And then through the window from the dark outside she heard a voice: "Princess? Princess? Are you there, Princess?"

"Who's that?" said the Princess, going to the window and looking out.

"I am the boy from the ford. I came to the gate to make my suit, but your father wouldn't let me in, saying that you would never marry. I have been waiting around and pining and sighing until it was dark enough to approach your window."

"Really?" said the Princess. "Let's hear you sigh, then?"

And the boy let out a sigh like a soft wind in the trees, so laden with longing that the Princess' heart went out to him.

"I can't see you," said the Princess.

"The moon is behind a cloud," said the boy. "Why don't you come down and we can walk in its light?"

"And how do I know that you will behave honourably?"

"Because, if I don't," said the boy, your father would track me down and inflict on me a horrible death."

"Good point," said the Princess, leaping out the window. The boy caught her (which was lucky) then set her down on solid ground.

"So, what are we going to do now?" said the Princess.

"Whatever you would like," said the boy.

"Well, I suppose since you put me down immediately when you caught me and behaved like a gentleman so far, we could walk together." And they started to stroll into the beech wood. "So," said the Princess. "Show me something like the other suitors showed me." The moon came out from behind a cloud, and the silver trunks of the beech trees under the moonlight almost glowed. The boy said: "What does the moon remind you of?" And the Princess looked, and thought, and then said: "It just looks like the moon."

"Look again," said the boy.

And the Princess said: "Oh!" Then in a still voice she added: "She is a woman going 'Oh!'"

"Why is she going 'Oh!'?" said the boy.

"Because she's just realized something."

"What has she just realized?" said the boy.

"That she's alone in the night sky with only a few stars far far away."

"Yes," said the boy. "And it's cold, and she knows she will set, and rise again tomorrow, but she's alone, and she wishes she could be with the sun, so busy is he with warming the earth and making the crops grow."

"Yes," said the Princess. "Show me something else."

"Look at the way the moonlight falls on that pond," said the boy. "What does that remind you of?"

And the Princess looked, and thought, then said: "A man waiting."

"Why is he waiting?"

"He's waiting for the moon to see him, and see that she's not alone, but when the moon looks at him, she only sees her own reflection." She stopped, and looked for quite a long time. Then she said, eagerly this time: "Show me something else."

"Behold the ford," said the boy, for they had reached it by now. And the Princess looked at the moonlight shining on the riffles as the water flowed over it, sparkling and alive. And she said: "Oh" and she smiled at him.

"What does it remind you of?" said the boy.

And the Princess, still smiling, said: "It's a river of diamonds."

And so they got married, and although the King tore the rest of his hair out, they lived a long time and had many children.

She looked at me like she was seeing me for the first time, then tilted her head and asked: "Are you trying to seduce me?"

"That, of course, is entirely up to you," I said.

But if I kept playing this out, the way things stood between us, things could never really get better. Anyhow, now there was all the time in the world..

I put the watermelon rind onto the plate and stood up. "Right now I should be going, though," I said. She nodded and looked at me oddly. I was thinking fairly odd thoughts about myself as well. I wasn't sure exactly what I was doing. But I had discovered some new strength. The trick in life, I thought, was to fill up every moment with the next best thing. And now was another moment.

"Oh! I forgot." I said. "I took one of your soaps, and meant to ask you if that was all right." Still a lie, but at least I was getting toward the truth.

"Oh, go ahead," she said absently, and stood up.

"They don't put them in the rooms where I'm sleeping," I said, and kissed her lightly on both cheeks.

She looked in my eyes. "Are you poor?"

"Yes. Very."

She considered this, but it seemed all right with her. "Tomorrow?"

"Sure."

"Come by in the morning," she said. "I'll see you in the lobby. There are a few things I have to get done, but if you're doing nothing else?"

"I'll be there."

On the way down to the lobby I thought that I really should just leave my manuscript for her to read: that would explain everything. But going back to her room now would only confuse things, so when I got to the front desk I asked whether I could have it sent up to Aurélie, and the man on duty said: "Certainly, sir," then gave me a manila envelope to put it all in and asked for her room number, which he wrote on the envelope and put in the correct cubbyhole behind him. I tipped him more than I could really afford, then thanked him and started toward the door. It was out of my hands now.

As I was walking across the lobby I heard a raised voice outside, looked up and saw something happening through the glass exit door, an argument between a girl and a man. It looked like he was getting the worst of it. She was stamping one foot and pointing with one finger at his chest, and he was making calming motions with his hands.

He was the Orange Man from the Essaouira bus.

I saw him before he saw me and, because it was too late to change direction, I adopted the expression of good grace I had left him with two days ago and pushed through the door. I was ready to pass by without acknowledging them, but he looked up and recognized me, though he couldn't remember from where. That didn't matter to him right now: *any*thing would be a distraction from this embarrassing public argument. He turned and said hello with a sudden big empty smile, turning attention away from the girl.

"Oh. Hello," I said, pretending not to have noticed that they had been arguing. "Are you here for the conference too?"

"What? Me? Oh. Hi. Hello. Yes."

The girl waited, then looked at me, then back at him, waiting for an introduction. He smiled and nodded, and then snapped out of it. "Oh," he said, turning to his girl, "This is ..." And then he remembered where he knew me from and turned back towards me, remembering that he wasn't supposed to be friendly to me, and his confusion was almost fatal. By pausing, it made her think that he had actually forgotten her name.

"My name is Hélène," she said in appalled disbelief. "I was with you on the bus from Essaouira. That was me. Remember?"

"Of course," I said.

"It's good *some*one does," she said.

"I re*mem*bered," the Orange Man said, like a stupid child. He was aware that he was making a fool of himself but was unable to stop. It must've been a nightmare. And she just let him suffer.

"I'm sorry," she said, turning to me. "We never actually caught your name ..."

"Yes," the Orange Man said, jumping in. "Hello."

"You already *said* that," said Hélène.

"Yes. But. (Not *now*, Hélène.) I would like to have a word with him. About work." He was trying to attain control, turning the steps of the hotel where he was losing into his office, where he had authority. He turned back to me. "If you would," he said. "Some business?"

It all sounded to me completely improvised, but I played along. "Of course."

"Just a word if you would."

And he pushed the door open and led me back inside, with the girl following.

"I'll get the key for the room," she said, turning away. Then: "I'll see you upstairs, Marcel."

Marcel.

I should have put it together before. But my surprise was easy to hide: he was too busy rattling on to even notice. "I'm glad I ran into you again because I'd like to talk to you about where you heard that story on the bus."

"Which one?" I said.

"What?" he said. He hadn't thought that far ahead.

"Which story? I told a bunch of them."

"That's partly what I want to discuss. It occurs to me that they make interesting examples of some of the types of stories which are of particular interest to me."

"Oh?"

"Yes. That is to say, what we call 'Parables of Absurdity.' I've cross-referenced the plot points with other similar stories from other cultures, and I think I have found enough matrices of similarity to justify further research. But I need more information on their origins." He was well on his way to being back on top now, blather fuelled by alcohol, which I could smell on his breath.

"I see."

"Well, it's very complicated," he said, though it wasn't, really. "Perhaps if you'd like to have a drink somewhere I could explain myself further."

"Sure."

"Fine. Now if I can just find out where *she* went," he said, turning to the left and so not seeing her coming around on his blind side. "I don't know why she does this. Every *time* ..."

"Every time what?" she said.

"Ah! There you are!"

"Yes," she said. She was not smiling.

"Well, I was just saying ..."

"Yes. I heard."

"Fine. So. We'll go have a drink, then ... You're welcome to join us."

"Well, *thank* you," she said, like she considered herself entitled to sit in without an invitation. "But no, thank you. I'll see you in the room."

"OK. See you then," he said, rather quickly, and she threw him a parting glare. "Women," he said conspiratorially to me. "Don't get me started ..."

But she had come back again, once more on his blind side. "Don't worry," she said. "I won't."

He jumped. "What? Oh yes. I was just saying ..."

"Yes. I *heard* you. Now. Do you have the toothpaste?"

"What toothpaste?"

"The toothpaste we just bought." She stood with her hand out, not letting him off the hook while he patted himself down and up again, checking all the pockets of his many-pocketed vest. Then he went through them again, taking everything out and holding it all in his hand. A small digital recorder, a monocular, tweezers, a comb, a note-pad, two pencils, a pencil sharpener, various crumpled Kleenex, a small Opinel knife, keys, and a small flashlight. "Didn't I already give it to you?"

"No."

"Are you sure? Because it's not here."

"Did you put it in your bag?"

"No, I remember I put it in my pocket," he said. "I remember."

"Obviously. And exactly which pocket?"

"It must've fallen out."

"Maybe it fell into the bag."

"It's *not* in the bag. I'd *know* if I *put* it in the *bag*, Hélène." Like she had been accusing him of feeble-mindedness.

"Well, it's not in the vest."

"Well, it's *not* in the *bag*. I'm *sure*."

There was a dangerous pause. And then Hélène snapped.

"Right. You're *sure*. Like you were *sure* about which direction to take in the souks." She leant in towards him and started gesturing with swift short stabs in the air, making very sure that she was being understood, back to the tableau I had seen through the glass door. "You were sure about that too, *weren't* you? And it wasn't possible that you were *wrong*. You simply *know. Everything.* You've *always* known everything. And how do you know *that*? Because *you* said it!" And with that she swore, stomped her foot, crouched quickly, looked in one pocket in the bag, then another, said: "There," and took out the tube of toothpaste. She stood up straight suddenly, glared quickly at him, held the toothpaste tube in front of his eyes, said: "I'll be upstairs," turned and stomped away.

He directed me in silence to the bar off the lobby, found a chair and sat down, putting on the table the handful of possessions from his pockets. "She put that toothpaste in the bag," he said. "For some reason she feels the need to create these scenes."

But she was back again. "And a toothbrush," she said, crouching down and finding it.

"Ah, Hélène. We were just ..."

"Yes," she said, "I *heard*." And left.

He waited this time, watching her till she was on the elevator and the door had closed.

So from my point of view, it was all very satisfying.

"Would you like a drink?" he said.

"Certainly," I said.

He nodded his head in the direction she had left. "She always accuses me of being self-centred, but *she's* the selfish one." He was nettled. "You can't *say* that of course. You're not *allowed* to say that. Because she's always *doing* things for other people. But I know for a fact that she only does it to *appear* like she's generous. So really she's only doing it for herself. I mean, how selfish is that? What about *me*?" He probably didn't know what he sounded like. "I mean *I'm* the one who has to get up tomorrow and read out a paper." He found his cigarettes, took one, lit it and inhaled. "And I haven't even written a damn thing." He glanced up to see if he was eliciting any sympathy from me, and I obliged him with a look of commiseration. "I meant to write it ... and the girl who usually helps get it done, well, that didn't work out ..." He let the thought drift away. That girl would have been Aurélie.

"So," I said, taking it up from when we had last talked. "Have you made it to the Djemma?"

"No. No, we haven't," he said. Then he smiled. "We've been ... otherwise occupied." He did his best to smile like Satan, Lord of the Underworld, as opposed to a greasy little man on a naughty weekend.

I feigned innocence. "Oh?" I said. "What have you been doing?"

And his face dropped at the thought that somehow he hadn't made clear to me the vast amount of sexual activity he'd been indulging in. "Oh, nothing ..." He retreated, then regained a bit of high ground. "Or actually, maybe I shouldn't divulge." And he positively leered.

I stared back vacantly and said, "Oh?" again, completely without inflection. It was a more effective ploy than the thorough beating he deserved. I recognized in myself the sudden dangerous strength of that feeling, but when the battle starts there is a singleness of purpose which comes as a relief, and maybe that's why there is war: as a vacation from the tension of maintaining a balance of power. I judged that I could conduct this skirmish without danger of falling over the edge into the abyss, by telling myself that I was aware of the dangers. Also, with Aurélie at my side, I was at the height of my powers. And he was a babbling idiot, asking sympathy from an almost complete stranger, and come to think of it, one who he'd met first as an enemy.

Then the drinks arrived and he pounced on his. So maybe that was it. I had thought that he had been purposely forgetting our confrontation on the bus because he needed my help, but maybe he was just so alcoholic that he didn't really remember clearly what had happened. I glanced at him closely, and saw that glassy lid behind the eye, that wall of fog. Was that how bad it was? A drunk in a Muslim country? But as pathetic as he could be, I had to remember the damage he was capable of doing. It would be best to stack everything in my favour now.

"How long does it have to be?" I said.

"What?"

"The talk tomorrow."

"Oh. Half an hour."

"*When a study is made of the Indo-European storytelling tradition,*" I said, "*one is struck by the woeful lack of attention which is paid to the nature of the audience.*"

"What?" He looked up. "Oh. Yeah. That sort of stuff."

"*And what is often forgotten, (or at least never seriously examined),*" I continued, "*is the effect the audience has on the story itself. The academic tradition is such that once a narrative is written down, it is seen to be cast in stone (as it were) but to the storyteller this is not always the case, and indeed almost never is.*"

Hope started to kindle in his eyes. "You've done this sort of thing before."

"Sure."

"Well, that's what I mean."

"*Certain parties have even gone as far to suggest that the narrative exists in a void, although any field experience at all would almost immediately prove the opposite. Others have approached the recognition of the audience as a regrettable fact, an impediment, but no one to my immediate knowledge has laid claim to the idea that they are a fundamental cornerstone of any oral literature.*" The trick is to find the right tone and a character to declaim it, and then just let the words fall into place. You have to imagine not what you are saying but who you are as you say it. Sometimes it's almost like the connection between the brain and the mouth is cut, and that that character is moving your lips like a ventriloquist moves the mouth of his dummy.

"Do you mind if ...?" He took from his vest his recorder. "'*Fundamental cornerstone ...*' you were saying ...?"

"Go ahead," I said, and then he set the bait himself, pushing the "on" button, testing and holding it towards me.

I paraphrased everything I had said so far, with embellishment, from the top.

"This is great!" he said. "But they'll want an example. How about that story you told on the bus?"

"The Goat in the Tree?"

"What? No. The first one. Something about how the mountains got there." He seemed to have an absolute genius for homing in on the mediocre. "I made some notes about it when I got home."

"I am honoured that you should think me worthy of study," I said.

"Yeah. Well. I have to find some way to write off that Essaouira jaunt, anyhow." He said it like he was deflecting the embarrassment for having said something generous, but actually, that *was* the point of the whole exercise. Some expenses were being questioned, and that's really why he was talking to me. Honoured, indeed. "If you tell me that you're involved with the conference I can write your drinks off on my cheat sheet."

"I am involved with the conference," I said.

"In what capacity?"

"None. I just said so because you asked me to."

"Oh. So ... why *are* you here, then?"

"Just visiting someone."

"Ah. Well. Tell me where you heard that story then. I can claim you as a source."

You can claim me as no such thing, I thought. I will not be caught in your web. But I said: "Well, let me think. I was in Montpelier, had just arrived by train from Marseilles that day. I remember because we passed into a tunnel and my ears popped at the same time as a lady's, who was sitting beside me in the train. We said 'Oh' at the same time and smiled at each other and started a conversation. It turns out she was from the same quarter in Paris as I was ..." An idea was starting to bloom about where to take this, but he interrupted me.

"The source was detected to be from Montpelier," he said into his recorder.

Which reminded me that I had work to do. "Yes. There's this guy who owns the café down by the train station."

"Which one?" Marcel's eyes lit up. "Café de la Place?"
So he knew Montpelier.

"Could be," I said. "I forget."

"Jules?"

"Maybe."

"Jules owns the Café de la Place. Large man. Handle Bar moustache?"

"I had quite a lot to drink that night."

"Anyhow, he told you the story?"

Not if you know him he didn't, I thought, and now it was time to leave Montpelier. "No. He told me about a boat to Finland."

"Finland?"

"Yes. It left from Bordeaux. His brother worked on it and they needed an assistant steward. So I went to Bordeaux, got the job onboard, set sail for The Hague, then up the Baltic coast to Helsinki. I jumped ship there, and worked in a lumber mill in the north, where I stayed with an old Sami guy."

"Sami?"

"Reindeer herder."

"What, like in a skin hut?"

"No. He was actually born in one of those, but this was one of those Government built houses. Plywood. Anyhow, he was a storyteller."

"What was his name?"

"Finn Siberling," I said without hesitation. "Great guy. One ear. Lost the other in a fight. Chewed off. Anyhow, that winter there was this big ice storm. The electricity went off, and we started telling stories. He went on for days, but still the storm went on. Until he was out of stories. No more? I asked. Well, there is one, he said. Then he told me that one."

"I see. Did he tell you where he heard it?"

"Sure."

He poised his pencil. Looked me right in the eye. "Where?"

"He saw it on television."

"What?"

"It was a movie he saw on television. I think it was a Turkish film."

He sighed. Took off his glasses. Sighed again. Put his pencil down.

"What's wrong?" I said.

"Can't use it."

"Why not?"

"It's not in the oral tradition."

"Sure it is. I told it to you."

"Doesn't count."

"I see. Well, that's where it came from, anyway."

"What am I going to do now?"

"How about that Goat in the Tree story?"

"Which one's that?"

I think he was only pretending he didn't know, trying to somehow erase his behaviour towards me on the bus. So I started sketching the story out for him again. He nodded like he remembered vaguely. I tried to make it as academic as possible and became dangerously close to draining all the blood out of it completely.

"Where'd you hear it?" he asked cautiously.

"I heard Aziz tell it." I might have to go see Aziz later about this in case Marcel went to check. Not too much of a worry about that, though. Marcel was probably not that energetic a collector.

"Aziz?"

"The bus driver. He told it coming down."

"But we didn't hear it coming down. You weren't on the bus."

"Last week, when I *did* come down," I said.

"Oh. Where did *he* hear it?"

"I think he said his Grandfather told it to him."

"His grandfather didn't have a TV, did he?" he said ruefully.

I smiled. "Doubt it. He's from way out in the desert somewhere."

"Hmm." I could tell he was starting to get interested.

"So," I suggested, "how about this?"

Take for example the absurdist parable which I collected on the bus from Essaouira, where I had gone on a tip from a contact here in Marrakech.

"That's good," he said. "I like that."

I had heard rumours of a story about the Goat In The Tree, and was interested in pursuing it to its source, but like so many stories, their springs are hidden from our sight. A story has a life of its own, and an unpublished one, passed from mouth to mouth, is of inestimable value to the study of folklore.

"Yes, that'll work, but now you need to work in some phrases like 'Narrative string' or 'Transmittable arc'."

"How long is the speech supposed to be?"

"A half hour."

"Shouldn't be a problem."

The bus tour takes 3 hours and the guide fills the time with dubious historical content. But when a young goat was spotted standing on the top branches of an argan tree, it reminded him of a story handed down from his Grandfather.

It was dangerously easy to write academic language, full of constructions which only someone who worked in a

university would write, not comprehensible without se-
vere concentration. As a comedian wants laughter, the
academic wants a roomful of people frowning and scowl-
ing at them with looks of strained concentration, so that
somebody seeing them would say: "They certainly are
thinking *hard*." The problem with writing that way, and
for the reasons I was doing it, was that the Muse moved
away. I saw her out of the corner of my eye and She
wagged her finger at me and clucked Her tongue in
disapproval.

And I, to my shame, turned a blind eye to Her and
swung back into the task at hand. This was politics. A
chess game. I was putting myself into position to either
block the enemy's move or destroy him. So I said my
spiel into the recorder and Marcel occasionally added
words and phrases from his world, which I included because they made him feel that the speech was his. When
we had finished, he had the makings of an original half
hour paper, ready for typing.

During all this he managed to act the part of someone who was still in charge, and I pretended to defer to
his authority. If I had allowed myself to think about it, I
would have been nauseated. As it was, I accepted the
role he had adopted for himself, that he *could* have done
it alone, just that he was temporarily too occupied and
distracted by the vast weight of his responsibilities.
Then he took out his wallet and, school out for the day,
he got on with his real vocation: drinking on a per diem.

As we drank we talked about Essaouira. A few times
he started to breach the topic of himself as a sexual ath-
lete, but I stared back blankly every time, so you could
tell that soon he was itching to leave, or have me leave,
so he could go sit over by the bar and buy more overpriced drinks for overaged playboys on expense accounts

which could be written off on the conference. All over the world in the bars of lonely big hotels, with lights set craftily low to hide the age of the clientele, lives were dripping away, and if it's all so meaningless anyway, why not get your little thrill? And if it hurts anybody, don't be so sensitive: it's *all* pointless, as everybody knows. *Every*thing was pointless. Except for alcohol.

After I left the hotel, his face was still in front of me, frightened, chain-smoking, looking for sanctuary or forgetfulness, hounded by the dogs of Hell. His face looked out from a narrow street off Mohammed Cinq as I walked by. It floated in the late evening air ahead of me, avoided looking in the mirror where it might see the age in its eyes. It hung around the Bab as I walked through. I saw it hiding in a doorway without a real friend, or even an art to sustain him.

But I had to remember that he was not only *self*-destructive. I once knew a guy who loved to drive at high speed. "If I'm going to die," he used to say, "it's going to be at 180 kph." He liked saying it. It made him seem devil-may-care. Then, sure enough, he had an accident, which he survived, in fact, walked away from without a scratch. He had killed an innocent bystander, however, a thirteen-year-old girl.

And telling myself that sad story I came to the park between the Djemma and the Koutoubia. The Square de Foucault was two rows of old trees with pounded earth between. Three huddled families were starting to lay out gear and lie down. I could always try and spend the night here as well. If I could wrap myself in newspapers on a park bench I'd be comfortable, though newspapers tend to keep you awake by rustling when you shift position, and anyway there were not many newspapers in Morocco, the literacy rate being low. Also, nowadays some park benches are built with unnecessary arm-rests designed to stop you from lying down on them at all, though those kind of benches were mostly back in France. Come to think of it, there was probably a connection between literate countries and countries with purposely not-too-useful park benches, but I wasn't thinking clearly enough to find one. My thoughts were popping around like a grasshopper.

Of course it was really not my business what Marcel does, or did, or whether he is a force for destruction which has to be stopped or a drunken buffoon who needed no help from me on his way down. There was no real justification to set him up like I did, but I am only my lady's servant, helpless before her. Her knight, standing vigil in this square, ready to do battle the next day. I thought of Rolland, blowing his horn "help! help!" while he backed himself into a corner in Roncesvalles, and how the night before he had gone to the garden of a chapel, and, while the moonlight shone on his armour, doffed and laid aside, he stood and thought about things. It seemed like a good idea. I didn't have a room anyway.

I thought about how I might die tomorrow. If the hotel had delivered the manuscript to her door and if she was still awake, she might have picked it up and was reading it already. Right now she might have finished the part about the party in Essaouira, then followed me onto the bus. Then the trip here to Marrakech and the part about sleeping in the baggage compartment, which might make me seem a bit crazy to her, but after all, it *did* all happen. Then the hotel swimming pool the next morning and the walk to the Djemma. Then she herself came into it, as someone deceived right from the beginning, and I was counting on her not to throw the manuscript out the window when she got to that point but to read on until my actions were justified. My guess was that she probably wouldn't be able to put it down by then, but it did no good to worry about it.

All I had, probably all I ever would have, was their attention. Just like Scheherazade. Keep them enthralled or they chop off your head.

I was tired but I didn't feel like sleeping. Traffic circulated around the park while brassy light the colour of Belgian beer, an argon lamp above the trees, cast shadows which would never move like moonlight, never mark time. I closed my eyes and wished there was a beach, like Essaouira, where I could stretch out shamelessly and get a good solid eight hours sleep. The noise of the Djemma gradually grew fainter, like a freight train full of tambourines slowly receding in the distance. I swayed, caught myself and opened my eyes again, then leant my back against a tree and squatted down. I checked my satchel for a plastic bag I knew I had, found it and wrapped the satchel in it, and sat on the satchel with my legs stretched out. Some sleep would mean I would be more capable the next day. Maybe Rolland had died the day after his vigil because he had been too tired to fight.

She'd have read the part about our first meeting at the Djemma by now.

A father of one of the families in the park glanced at me, then immediately looked away, puzzled at what I was doing here: with clothes like mine, I could obviously afford a hotel room. I thought I'd like to give them something, but what did I have except a few stories? They'd heard stories all their lives. Money was what they needed. They were homeless, in from some village east of here. The husband had been a truck driver, then he'd broke his foot and was no good to the company who had hired him. Then twice as much rain had fallen last year and their mud-brick house had started to dissolve ... And there I go again. It's just a habit I can't kick.

Across the street a guarded gate opened and a couple emerged, dressed in clothes bought specially for the vacation from their jobs up north, down here on the two weeks off that their contract allowed. I caught myself thinking that it's not their fault, they just think that money will help. And it will help, too, if you don't have any. More money than enough, though: that just distracts you. How nice not to be them, I thought. And if they looked at me they probably would have thought that I was either some poor guy down on his luck, or perhaps that I deserved it, that I'd made my choices and were living with the consequences. Wealth, I've always observed, hardens one's opinions.

Then the couple turned and I saw for the first time the face of the man who looked exactly like a guitar player I once knew, and it got me thinking back to where I'd seen his look-alike, in Paris, last autumn, on Rue St Grégoire de Tours. I closed my eyes and could see it all again.

WAS LOOKING through the window into a bar. It was dark inside, with a splash of light in one corner glinting on a microphone stand. I entered from the street into a room with a low ceiling held up by big oak beams, inexpertly joined, but massive and solid.

It was Tuesday, a slow night. A large bored bartender looked up from wiping a glass that didn't need it. I went to the bar and ordered an overpriced beer. They needed more customers to stay open and the staff was probably ready to bolt if offered work elsewhere, but the waitress came over and tried to pretend otherwise. I said I was fine with just the beer. Somebody looked in, saw that nothing was happening, and moved on. The guitar player came over and I nodded to him. I believe he was thinking that if he sat with me and talked he wouldn't have to perform.

"Played here long?" I asked.

"First time," he said. "I'm doing it as a favour to René. His regular act skipped out at the last minute."

Failing businesses are all the same. But I like it down there, to tell the truth, because at the times you have nothing else, you need spirit. It forces you to get in touch with the source.

"Usually I'm up at the Canal St. Martin," he said. "Three nights a week. Good crowds, big tips." He looked around. "Here? They don't advertise. Look at this!" And he took a stack of flyers off the bar. "What good are these doing *here*! Somebody should be handing them out on the street. If you get a crowd through the door, I can keep them in." I saw that dream in his eyes. A line-up on the street and a waiting expectant audience who, just to get onstage, you'd have to pick your way through like an over-abundant kitchen garden.

"I'll go and hand these out if you pay for this beer," I said.

He considered it. "What do I have to lose?" he said. "I get two free beer anyway."

I took a stack of flyers and walked out on St Grégoire de Tours and up a block to St Germain des Prés, where I caught a passerby's eye and handed him one. He waved it away. The second passerby did the same. The third took it, glanced at it, and dropped it in a garbage can. I mimed my disappointment operatically. A young couple, arm in arm, laughed at my performance but passed on. A head turned at the sound of their laughter: I caught his eye and smiled. He smiled back. I handed him one. He took it and read it as he walked away. I fanned the handbills out like playing cards, wrinkled my nose and glanced to the left and the right suspiciously, then rearranged my hand, pulled one from the right side of the fan and placed it in the left, all for another couple walking toward me. As they passed I placed it in the girl's hand and then turned to the next. Fanning with my make-believe hand of cards with exaggerated boredom, I exhaled hugely and handed one to them, surprisingly, from around behind my back. The art of mime has been formalized, taught in schools and then brought back to the street, cluttered up with notions about how it should be done, so it has lost its naturalness, but how else do you get a story across to a crowd with no common language?

I worked that corner till two thirds of the flyers were gone, then walked down to the Buci, which is narrower and crowded and a more difficult place to operate. By this time it was the late night pedestrian rush hour. I went back to the bar where there were half a dozen couples now, three of them from groups I had handed flyers to. The guitarist was wondering whether he should go on, whether there were enough people to form the critical mass which makes for an audience, and not just a few embarrassed patrons. The bartender looked surprised to see me back. But something was starting to happen. You could feel the first faint knitting together of trust, like the caul that covers a seed before it sprouts, the first charge of magnetism as the ions jostled for alignment and pulled together.

One couple got up and left. The others you could see were wondering if they should leave before it started, when it would be harder to make the break.

"When's your next set?" I asked the guitar player.

He looked at his watch. "It's supposed to be now, but the crowd's not big enough." And I thought: how is it supposed to get that big, if nothing's going on?

"I'll introduce you, if that's OK. Some of them already know me."

"Sure," he said, nervous, but hiding it.

I stood up and tucked the remaining flyers in my breast pocket where they flapped over comically and bobbed and waved with my movements like some sea frond in the surf. Then I walked to the stage.

Large speakers like the obelisks at Carnac stood imposingly on either side. The microphone stuck out toward me like a giant insect's eye. But sound gear is a huge unwieldy problem, heavy to carry, ruled over by technocrats at every level, and even on the rare occasions it works perfectly, it only finally separates you from the audience, makes you, no matter how loud, easier to ignore. So I didn't even turn on the microphone.

Seated in the room were two couples from Norway or Denmark, one who remembered me as the guy who handed them the flyer that brought them here, and some Americans. But I had heard them order in French so Basic French was what was called for: "Welcome. Thank You. Show." I pointed to the stage I was standing on and addressed a questioning look at them. In a new situation when people don't know how to behave, if you act as though you *do* know, their eyes are naturally drawn to you.

They nodded back. Nice people, but wondering what they'd got themselves into. I went back into the silent comedian character I had performed on the street, straightened up and tapped a finger at my chest in a parody of self-importance, then preened my feathers. "Ladies and Gentlemen," I said. As though I was translating, but only really saying it with the accents of a German, an Italian, and a Chinese. "Ladies and Gentlemen, *Ladies and Gentlemen*, LADIES AND GENTLEMEN." I stopped, and swept my arm to indicate the glories of this cellar. "Great Pleasure. You. Us. Here. Tonight." All with different accents. I let this sink in, then continued. "Now!" I pointed at the microphone and the guitar on its stand beside the stool. I raised my eyebrows up and nodded slowly like this was going to be really something. I gestured again, tilted my head closer like a secret not just everybody was lucky enough to be let in on, and said in an exaggerated whisper: "Guitar!" I followed this with more nodding. But they weren't ready yet, and neither was the guitar player. I held up one finger as though to silence them and with a flourish drew three flyers out of the remaining pack in my breast pocket.

I held them up so they could examine them, both sides, then smiled like a donkey at nothing. I rolled the three flyers into a tube, blank on the outside. I looked through it like a telescope, to show that it was empty. I made a lion roar through it, which coming from such a small tube, made quite an effect. I jumped back and grinned like a donkey again at the thought of having frightened myself. They laughed. I held the paper tube up and gazed at it with one raised eyebrow and pursed lips like a scientist with a test tube, then delicately ripped one edge down halfway. "Now ..." I said and made a drum-roll sound with my lips and signalled that they should join in. They did, and as the drum-roll continued, I ripped three other edges down, raised a finger for them to build a crescendo, added a voice trumpet of a rising chord and, with all my attention on the tube of paper, I pulled the inside out and up so that the ripped ends flopped open into a flower. Because I had rolled it with the printed side in, it made a pleasing effect of surprising colour when the petals flopped open.

I bowed deeply to the applause, swept one arm out, and said: "Guitarist!" Amid continued applause, I stepped offstage, and, still in the full spotlight, first gestured for permission from her boyfriend, then handed the paper flower to the girl seated at the nearest table. She gestured back with a seated curtsey, and I walked away from the stage into the shadows. Once out of the light I could see the number of people in the seats had grown by two and there was a group of what looked like five at the door who had watched this performance and was just deciding to come in.

I went towards the bar. The bartender was nodding his head approvingly. This was not going to be like the other nights. It still wouldn't be profitable, but the downward spiral was slowing. He drew a beer for me, put a slice of lemon on its edge, then made a motion like he was toasting me. I thanked him. He smiled and winked. I watched a lemon seed which had fallen out of the wedge into the beer sink to the bottom, and then as the tiniest of bubbles gathered around it, floated to the surface where the bubbles popped, and the seed sank again. That's what it feels like. You touch bottom, then let yourself float up again, laughing.

Meanwhile the guitarist had stepped on stage and, without acknowledging the audience, sat down, put his guitar in his lap, then craned around and flicked a switch on an amplifier behind him. He strummed, and hearing nothing come out of his speakers, craned around his other side, pushed a button on a smaller pre-amplifier, and strummed again. He tapped the microphone and clicked more switches. Now he had sound, but apparently it didn't meet some standard or other, so he twiddled some knobs and strummed again. He did this seven or eight times. So far, not much of a show. When he was satisfied as to the quality of the tone, timbre and parametric equalization, he then started to tune the guitar. All this he could have been shaping into a performance, instead he was only getting ready. The audience waited for some punch line, became aware that there wouldn't be one, and since nothing of interest was happening on stage, started to talk amongst themselves.

But I shouldn't be rough on him. His art was in a dark studio somewhere and a row of lights and knobs. I am sure he could paint a beautiful picture there. He misunderstood his function here, was all. I didn't.

Finally he started into his first song, which show-cased the mathematical element of music rather than its value as a communicator of emotion. He'd lost the audience. But they didn't seem to mind. They were talking, not listening, but at least settling in for another drink.

After a short set and a few more songs, he put his guitar back onto its stand and stepped off stage. I got up and did another turn.

And I could have gone on all night. It turned out they knew quite a lot of French if I stayed away from the idiom. So I spoke more, which I'm better at anyway. I told them a story about my ride down to the bar on the metro that night, took them through it, my nose wrinkling at the smell of urine at the metro entrance, then onto the escalator, my hand on the rail slowly moving behind me. I waited on the platform and was buffeted as the train arrived, squinted at the squeal as it came to a halt, waited for the door to slam open, squeezed on just in time, made a psst! sound as the doors closed, but my backpack was caught outside the door, pinning my shoulders back. I stupidly stared as the metro started up again, arrived at the next station, halted with a hiss, the doors opened and I was freed, but now my shoulders were permanently pulled back. I tried to hold onto a strap as the metro started up again, but couldn't raise my hand that high. I swayed and stumbled around the car. Finally I got off at my stop and walked out and through the Sixth Arrondissement and ended the story by coming through the door of the bar, walked on stage and started to perform the first thing I had done that night. Pure autobiography plus exaggeration, memory in a circus hall mirror. I swear I even saw the guitarist smile.

And as always when things clicked, it was contagious. The waitress had it too now, her movements both efficient and friendly. She had euro notes of pre-determined denominations folded in her knuckles for easy access when making change, and coins in a leather pouch with three pockets, one for euros, one for two-euro pieces, and one for smaller coins.

It was a good night. There were other better nights to come, but that first was the one I remember, when the ice thawed and started the break-up. "Débâcle" shouldn't be a negative word. We'd found something, tapped into some spirit. I don't know what it is, but it's unmistakable when it happens: something to do with Time. Moments are filled and connected. And who cares if somebody else is getting something from it? That's what it's for, and when things start working there's more than enough for everybody. It felt good. That awful downward settling of failure as the clock ticks on, that feeling was banished, at least for a while.

Then it was time to close up. Thank you, good night. Applause. Lovely smiling people filing out slowly. Chairs put upside down on tables. Cash register calculating. The tips actually weren't that great, but if this kept up they would be. The waitress took them and spilled them onto the bar, with that sudden sound of pouring money, metallic, military. It glinted, and so did our eyes. That might have been when things started to go wrong.

"Tomorrow night?" said the bartender.

"Certainly," I said, and I took the metro back to my garage in the Buttes aux Cailles.

That week business increased steadily. By the weekend we were almost full. Monday we were closed, Tuesday, while giving handouts, somebody waved me away and said: "We're already going." And after that I didn't need to hand out any more, though to tell the truth, I didn't mind. It was just another stage to work.

Now I hung around the bar between sets, which I probably shouldn't have done. Everything that was happening there became part of what I knew and so it was either bound to creep into my work, or else become a subject to avoid. And you can't afford to have too many of those, if you do what I do.

Also, there was the guitarist. As soon as he started to play, the audience would start talking. He would turn his volume up, and the audience would talk louder. This would go on through his set, so when I got onstage and turned the microphone off, it was like a breath of oxygen, which was fine for me, but my success was showing him up and creating tension. I wanted to tell him that anyway there was always only some tiny difference between clicking and failing, and that it wasn't his fault, that his craft was as strong as mine, just temporarily out of fashion. But I couldn't broach the subject because that would mean he would have to admit that he was failing. Also, he was responding to his situation by getting angry at the audience, taking it out on *them*, and that is almost always fatal.

Then there was the bartender, who was starting to put moves on the waitress, feeding off the growing excitement in an attempt to bed her. She was avoiding him by doing her job more efficiently, spending more time out on the floor serving customers, making sure she always had something to do. He was trying to be charming to her, but I had the impression that as soon as it became clear that this wasn't working, there would be little injustices, demands for pointless additional tasks, and withholdings of tips to corner her into doing what he wanted. Already he was asserting his authority by criticizing the guitarist, and making veiled threats about getting rid of him if he didn't hold the audience better.

Things around the edges were getting ugly. With success had come self-interest.

One night someone came in who didn't seem to be there either for the entertainment, or because we were becoming the place to be seen. There was something professional about him, and he invited me to sit with him and his friends before the show. They mentioned that they had all individually been in before and found my work interesting.

"Thank you," I said. "That's what it's for."

They were very polite and complimentary, but I could tell that perhaps its simplicity bothered them, and its popularity. Accessible to everybody, it was a tiny bit suspect. My guess was that they were the sons and daughters of international parents, the offspring of families of art profiteers who'd raised them on theories and history, movements and breakthroughs, with opinions on how art should be practiced, created and presented, all those things which were deadly to the creation of the things themselves. They were on the lookout for the Next Big Thing. And even if it wasn't as noble as they would like, it could be profited off, to fund more worthy and exclusive projects. And if it turned out that they had backed the right horse, arguments later could always be supplied to justify it.

And why not? I had my craft, they had theirs. I did find myself thinking though that perhaps it would be better if they were just involved with the money, not attempting to shape public taste as well. The next set I told a story about a man who got rich but found that he couldn't buy anything of real worth. Afterwards I sat with them again as, politely and respectfully, they picked it apart. I thought as I listened that it was a good thing that I didn't have to tell it again. The baggage it had accumulated just by listening to them criticize it would make it almost impossible to perform. I've always found that it was almost always easier to just make up new ones, anyway.

But the man who had introduced himself to me was impressed, and it was just my luck that he was a critic with a column in a small giveaway over on the Oberkampf. The next week, I saw my name in print, or at least the name I was using then. The crowds became larger. Tips were bigger. Everything was working. And there were times on stage when I could do no wrong, or rather, every wrong thing became surprising information which altered the direction of the story, and gave me another thread to follow. Things opened up in front of me on their own.

And right about then a new character came onto the scene.

One night I came off stage after my first set and I saw the bartender over by the door eagerly agreeing with someone. The owner. A monthly visit to a failing investment which had surprised him by having become a flourishing enterprise, and he was here to re-establish his control. The bartender introduced me to him. He complimented me on my act, but did not neglect to give me the impression that he was, make no mistake about it, the boss. My boss. What he said went. Because he said so.

After the bar closed up he invited me into a miniscule office off the kitchen and started to negotiate some sort of arrangement with me. He told me that this was just a discussion to see what my plans were, but it was a deal he was after. So I couldn't tell him the truth, which was that I would do this for free, and that it was indeed this very attitude which allowed me to make the work valuable. He was a businessman, though, his fate was to control the money. His eyes flicked up at me and I glimpsed a memory of a slow-moving shepherd I had once seen, strolling to close an opening in the fence to cut off a sheep's escape. What a world we lived in, I thought, where victory went to the best deceiver.

So already we were into it. He suggested a photographer, and a poster outside, as an enticement for me. I didn't show it, but the idea terrified me. His parting words were that he'd get a friend of his to write up a contract, as a mere formality, you understand, for me to sign. Gates were being set up to herd me into smaller fields. Finally a field so small it was really a chute, with only one exit. So now there was something else to avoid.

His visits became nightly. The guitar player was starting to circle toward him, actually *looking* for a contract. The owner and the bartender would stand over by the bar, surveying the full house, satisfied.

"Look at them," the waitress said to me one night. "You'd think they'd done something right." She smiled at me and shrugged her shoulders at the folly of humans, then rolled her eyes as the bartender broke away from the owner and called her name. She heard him, acknowledged him, then suddenly turned away to a customer, professional again, avoiding the bartender by suddenly having too much to do. She had made the decision to do her job and only her job, and the choice had given her the freedom to think and say what she wanted.

I wondered if I could honestly say the same any more. I couldn't tell the story of the guitar player, who had started to hate me. I couldn't tell the story of the owner, or the critic and his friends, how, with all the advantages in the world, that freedom had yoked them, how the rich were fated to be cruel, how failure hurt them harder because they had no excuse to behave as they did.

Neither could I tell the story of the bartender, how, almost against his will, he was drawn toward the waitress, how although he knew she was rejecting him, he still had to approach her, demand her attention, and finally use his position to try and corner her. How he hated himself for that and how finally he hated her for that, but how he was still drawn to her, to prove to himself he was a good man. How the stakes he kept raising were inevitable in their outcome. How a manipulative man afraid of the passing years was really just another romantic swain. How to him she was the only thing that made sense. You could make from all that a beautiful story, with a looming inevitable crisis that needed only the surprising last detail, terrible and real.

I couldn't tell any of the stories woven out of the world I was living in, and although I was still able to hold the audience, and, though with less and less frequency, surprise them in ways they had not been surprised before, it was no longer effortless. A good performance spins along on oiled ball bearings, and this is not just self-indulgence to make things easier for myself, but a condition for quality.

I was coming up every night with four sets on the spot, although the fact that I was starting to count them should have told me that something was getting ready to collapse. On my last night there, the contract was ready to sign, the photographer was ready to snap my picture after the show, another journalist from one of the more established papers had been invited, and there was even talk of a television crew coming down. I stepped onto the stage and people started to turn toward me and quiet down.

I left my garage in the Buttes aux Cailles and walked to the metro in that cold fog we had tonight. Where did that fog come from? Did you feel it, coming here?

They nodded.

I took the metro to Sorbonne, and then, because I had an errand to run in Vavin, I thought I would cross through Luxembourg Gardens, so I walked across the Boul' Mich' and entered the south gate just before they closed for the night. Everybody was leaving, bustling back to their warm hives, bread under their arms, scarves wrapped high around their necks. I felt like a fish swimming upstream.

   By the time I reached the boat pond there was so much fog I could only just see the duck house in the middle and I had to search for those steps up to the tennis courts. It was getting dark now as well, darker than it should have been at this time of night ... well, you remember what it was like.

And they nodded again because they had seen it that evening on the way to the show. We were in the same world.

I made for Vavin, and it was getting almost supernaturally dark now, and I suddenly got the idea that I would be caught inside the park for the night, and I panicked a bit, and started to turn back, then walked and came out in a different place than I thought I would, which threw me off. I turned back, looked around, turned again, and now I was completely lost. I don't know how it happened. The fog didn't help, of course, I couldn't see my hand in front of my face, but it was more than that. It was eerie, like some groundless fear, which is more frightening because it was groundless.

And I thought I might play up the panic here, running in circles, but the story wasn't connecting up in that direction. It was starting to have the feel of a dream.

And I came to a gate which was closed, and walked along the fence keeping the railing on one side, and suddenly realized that I had been walking in the completely wrong direction, and so I crossed the entire gardens again, and the fog seemed to get even thicker now, and eventually I found myself next to the Orangerie, and nobody was around, and I knew I was too late to go run my errand on Vavin now, but I didn't want to go to the railing and yell for a policeman, because I was probably breaking the law just by being there now, and then I started to panic again. So when two cops came through, one with a machine-gun, I hid from them behind a huge plane tree, and it was absolutely dark now as well as foggy, and I waited, and snuck out of my hiding place and there was no way I could climb the iron railings, so I walked over to the Sénat, and found a door, put my hand to the knob ... and it was open, which must've been a mistake on someone's part, so I pushed it open and walked in, and I found myself in a dark hall. And now I was really nervous, because if they found me they would probably arrest and execute me as a terrorist.

And I stopped here, because the way this story was going, the only way I could see me getting out of it was to meet the President, and then having to hold him hostage just to get out of the building, make a comic heroic parody, a cheap trick. I was behind the wave of my own creation, faking it ...

And then, on stage there that night, I came to the edge of something. I realized with an empty dread that all the holes in the fences had been closed off, except the one where they wanted me to go.

So instead I said: "I'll take a break now." And I walked off stage and the audience started slowly talking again, some asking what was going on, some with concern, God bless 'em, because they saw that I had failed.

The owner was there by the bar, and he was concerned too, though for a different reason. He had an enterprise to run, and he didn't want to risk losing an audience. He signalled for me to come over and I hesitated before I went. I was not a dog to be whistled to. It annoyed me, and then I was annoyed at myself for being annoyed. While moving along the bar toward him, I tried to look like everything was under control, then it occurred to me with some surprise that frankly I didn't care anymore. And that, of course, was the real problem.

He gave me some advice. They may not know how to do it, but everybody knows when you flop.

"You should tell the one you told two nights ago," he said.

"Yes," I said, though I had no such intention. You see? I hadn't even realized how deep I was into it.

"The one about the American at the Eiffel Tower."

"Yes," I said. "It worked well." Which was true, but it was such an obvious story. Since I had told it I had been trying to forget it.

"Do it next set," he said. And it was no longer advice.

So when the time came to go back on, as I took my beer and threaded my way between the tables and chairs toward the stage, I thought I might tell instead a story about an army officer who told his scout where to look and how the scout first tried to accommodate him, although he knew the enemy wasn't likely to be bivouacked there, and how when this was proven to be true, how this information showed the officer up, and how his anger caused him to send the scout out on more and more dangerous patrols. That story could go some-where, but at best it would only teach him something, and insofar as a story does that, a less story it is. So no, not that one. What one then?

And suddenly I fell through some structure. It felt exactly like that, like all this time I had been constructing a scaffolding over an empty space, and now I fell through and there was nothing else but falling. I could actually feel myself turning in mid-air. A sudden swoop of fear and despair as what I was standing on collapsed and I felt like praying, to tell the truth, repeat some chant, some habit of words, though a mere habit would never be enough. My lips could move all I wanted, if they didn't touch my heart it was simply impossible. I needed some seed-crystal of meaning dropped into the super-saturated liquid around me, which would grow around it a marvellous shape, ordered and beautiful.

I stepped onto the stage, and I was tired, and I wanted to get home. I wanted to get back to my garage in the Butte aux Cailles, or take the TGV out to the Loire. In two hours I'd be there. Maybe I should describe how that felt while I was inside the Sénat in my story. And from the stage I looked out over the heads of the audience and outside the large window behind them I saw that it was starting to snow, big fat flakes illuminated as they fell through the cone of light from a lamp on the street. Nobody else saw it because they were all looking at me, and I realized how I could end my story and end this part of my life all in one. And in the tone of voice like someone who was trying to figure things out, I started where I had left off.

I walked in the dark down the corridor, and saw ahead of me a window, and I looked out and now it was snowing, big fat flakes, and there was one doorway I tried ...

The guitar player had put beside his chair on a small table a carafe of water, and as I talked I absently picked off bits of the foil label of the beer bottle I was carrying and dropped them piece by piece into it where they individually twinkled to the bottom. I had to stretch the story now, so in my story I tried the door but made it so it didn't open, then saw another door with a light under it, which switched off, and not knowing whether there was somebody behind or whether the light was on a timer, I tried it, and then saw a third. Something would have to happen now, so the third door in my story opened and I found myself in a huge high-ceilinged room with, in the far wall, a window, and, for later, a metal ladder leaning precariously beside the window where a workman had left it, unsafe. With everybody watching, I put the palm of my hand over the mouth of the carafe, and turned it upside down:

And the snow had turned into a blizzard.

And the bits of foil fluttered around obligingly and dramatically, and there was an ooh from the audience:

And I moved toward the window, and then I thought I heard a noise, like a piano, so I jumped to the side, and hit my head on something and it toppled toward me and I fell down, out cold. And the cat who made the noise walked across the piano keyboard, hopped off and came over and sniffed at me lying there unconscious.

They didn't question how, if I was unconscious, I would know that, and they must've figured out on their own that it was the falling ladder that I had hit my head on, but it didn't matter. I had them. All the same, I was slipping. It really was time to leave.

And as I lay there, outside the snow kept falling, piling up. It covered the ground, first melting as it hit, then falling too quickly to melt, as the ground turned from wet dark to white. And it kept piling up, and piling up, like words in a story. And everybody thought, how lovely, and the next day it was still snowing, filling the streets in huge smooth troughs like bobsled runs, and still it snowed, and it was quiet, because there was no traffic. The metro rumbled underground at first, but once the entrances were filled up, nobody went into them and the metros stopped running. And still it snowed. So when I woke with a sore head in the Sénat, the sun was shining through the window and everything outside was blinding white, trees buried up to their second branches, one arm of a high statue sticking out holding a sword. I walked to the window and tried to see if it would open, and it did. Snow was piled right up to the sill. I tested it with my foot to see if I would sink and found that it had crusted over so I could walk on it. I stepped out and it squeaked slightly as I stepped away, and now the alarm rang, but nobody was around so I just kept walking, across the much more beautiful Luxembourg Gardens, a smooth white pure vast coverlet, rolling in one long wave right up to the Boulevard Montparnasse and when I reached there I didn't stop, just walked on the snow right over the top of the iron railings it had buried, hard iron buried in bright snow, and across the Boulevard and up to the Observatoire. I could see people in second floor apartments looking out and some of them smiled and some even waved.

And the faces I saw in the story now were the faces of the audience looking at me.

And they looked back, allies in the appreciation of the wonderful. And then it started to snow again over all this loveliness, making it that much lovelier.

And the snow I saw falling in the story was the same as what I saw out the window behind them.

And still it snowed. It snowed and snowed like ... like ...

And I stumbled. But I knew what I was doing now, and it was done for effect. It worked exactly the way it should, too, because they were more attentive than they had ever been. I let the pause stretch. A chair squeaked with the sound of "ache!"

The snow fell like, there, like that ...

And I pointed and everybody in the audience, as well as the owner, bartender and waitress at the bar, looked around and some said "oooh." And, when they looked back, the stage was empty.

I had slipped offstage and into the kitchen. I could hear the rising bustle of their voices, but I walked through and out and stepped into the alley, and the door closed quietly behind me and then I couldn't hear them any more.

Outside the bar it wasn't like in my story. The snow fell but disappeared as soon as it hit the black pavement. The alley came out on Rue de L'Ancienne Comédie, and I turned right up to St Germain des Prés and took the metro to Place D'Italie. On the way out of the metro there, I saw a travel poster of a Touareg tribesman beside a camel and I stood and looked at it for a good long while. With the snow falling on the poster it seemed to me that he must be cold.

Time to go. I hadn't picked up my money for tonight, but I had saved enough over the last few weeks, and if I lived cheaply it would last me through winter. What good is freedom if you don't use it?

When I got to my garage, I packed my satchel then I took the metro to Alésia and a bus to Orly. I left my winter jacket at the airport and took a flight to Marrekech.

I stayed in Marrakech for a week, but heard it was cheaper to live on the coast, so I took a bus to Essaouira where I rented a room for the winter, with the wind over the medina playing a deep bass note like a giant flute. The air was gritty when the winds came but the room was large for what I was paying, and I ate good basic food from the region: fish, goat, oranges and almonds. In the spring I paid the last of my money for what I owed on my room and walked out onto the street carrying everything I owned in my satchel. I slept on the beach that night, and the next morning I swam in the ocean. I came out of the water, carrying my wet clothes which I had just laundered in the sea. I walked slowly up to the sea-wall above the tide line, laid my clothes out neatly on the wall to dry and, when they had, I donned them, walked back to the main street, and through the Bab, not knowing quite what to do next. A June breeze was blowing in from the sea, over the ramparts from the north, but it was calm here in the medina. And that's when I smelled that cooking from across the street.

ND NOW I was back in Marrakech and I hadn't slept at all and it was going to be a hot day. I got to my feet, dusted myself off, and moved down toward the Koutoubia. Morning light was tinting the eastern sky like tempering metal, but to the west, once away from the lights, you could see Cassiopeia, doomed to ride in her chair for eternity around the North Star, and Venus and Saturn strung along their elliptic. Darkest blue with stars, crystal specks on velvet. Marrakech was still a desert town.

Marrakech is still a desert town.

It had been a stupid idea to try to sleep leaning up against a tree. I had spent the night in a half-world of scattered thoughts which didn't link up into something bigger, and now I was up, blinking like an owl and starting to feel rumpled and scratchy, without the easy smile and swinging step, and someone in my position can't afford that. You have to be at the top of your form when you're at the bottom of the heap.

I needed a place to stretch out, three hours would do it. There were many small cheap hotels around town, but I didn't have the money. If there was a library somewhere I could take down a book from the shelves and slouch in a chair with it, but there weren't any public libraries in Marrakech that I'd ever seen. The railway station might have benches, but they might not, and it was too far to go just to find out. Maybe I could go to a hospital, walk up to the reception desk, say: "Excuse me ..."

—and collapse. They'd probably let me lie down for a few hours. I seriously thought about it.

By this time I was in the gardens by the Saadian Tombs and, to my side, squared-off mimosa shrubs lined straight walks with short benches without backs spaced alongside. If I lay along the length of one I might get a quick snooze so I sat down and pretended to tie my shoelace, but when I tightened it, it snapped. I started to undo the lace to repair it and discovered that there was one knot there already, craftily hidden behind an eyelet. I couldn't pull it through the hole, so I had to undo the entire lace. I wasn't thinking straight, because when I tied the broken ends together, with its two knots now I couldn't replace it through the eyelets, so I undid the knot I had just made and retied it, then threaded the other end through and made a knot while it was in the shoe, like a surgeon tying a suture, hiding it as best I could. I wouldn't be able to tighten it, but it would do for now. Then I retied the other shoe overhand the same way to look like everything was intended and I discovered that that lace was about to snap as well. This could become serious.

Irritated, I lay back along the bench with my head on my satchel. And of course I couldn't get to sleep. Thoughts kept popping into my head, and I had no peace. The day was starting to get hot, too, and the bench I had chosen was now in the sun. The morning call to prayer sounded from the Koutoubia, and I thought I could maybe file in with the devout, where at least it would be cooler, but I could not think how I could get any sleep out of it. I sat up and looked around for a bench in the shade, saw one with nobody on it and got up and walked toward it to claim it. Just as I got near, though, a lady sat down on it and I walked back to my original bench, but by that time somebody had taken it as well. I walked up and down the straight paths of the Gardens, but now there were more people here and the benches were filling up. Yesterday everything seemed possible, today nothing was going right. It could have been so easy. I could be lying in her arms now. And her bed was huge. And there was a pool at the hotel, and room service. I was starting to pity myself and forget the reasons I hadn't stayed with Aurélie, but what had I been thinking? Since when had the truth helped anything? All the truth does is make you unpleasant to be around. And who said I even knew what the truth was, anyway? Pure egotism and self-delusion. People just want distraction, and I, of all people, should know that. I've seen their faces as I trundled out the stories. And what in God's name made me think she was different than them? Because she was good-looking?

I was pacing now, and I didn't know why. I could feel the sun like a heat-lamp on my neck and shoulders and the stillness of the morning was like a bent dry stick just before it snapped. Then, a tiny wind moved on the path like an invisible broom making one small sweep, and in front of my foot, a laurel leaf flipped over. A pause, and like a flock of birds high up, a sudden dust storm came over from the direction of Aurélie's hotel, a narrow pillar of dirt whirled in crazily and hit my face and struck my eyes, forcing me to close them. The grimace I made exposed my teeth to it. I shut my lips and it got in my nostrils. People around me pulled their robes close to them, left the paths of the gardens and crowded into bushes, looking face inwards. It passed as quickly as it had come, and everybody moved back to the benches. When I had stopped squinting and the dust was out of my eyes I was still without a place to lie down, so I started to walk to Aurélie's Hotel, even though it was still early.

I walked up to Mohammed Cinq and through to the Gueliz. It seemed farther to get to the hotel than the night before, but I finally reached the front gate, not at all sure I should risk walking in. An employee in the booth examined me longer than normal as I passed. It was getting hard to keep up the façade. I entered the lobby, and turned quickly away when I saw behind the counter the same man who had been there two days ago. I don't think he saw me as I quickly crossed the floor and then down the hall to the side. I looked behind, seemed in the clear, then ducked into a washroom.

It was on a grander scale than the bathroom in Aurélie's room, but with the same abundance of towels and lined with the same exotic wood. I looked at myself in the mirror and could see what the man in the booth had been worried about. The dust storm had left a fine haze of powder on my face like poorly applied make-up and my eyes were red and rheumy. Behind my ears and on the inside of my nostrils it felt gritty.

I ran water and adjusted the taps, lovely brass fixtures with turned wood handles. The warm water felt very good washing the dust off. From a fluffy neat pile beside the sink I took a washcloth. It was greyish-red with dirt before I finished, so I soaked it and wrung it out thoroughly. Word could get around. I stood back from the mirror and examined myself again. My clothes were starting to look rumpled, but so were the clothes of any number of academics staying currently in the hotel. I could do with a haircut, but so could many of them. It was my beard which was the problem. I can go a day with no shaving, but two days and it definitely starts to look like I don't have a job. I took out my razor from my miraculous satchel, washed it under the tap, and soaped my face down with soft soap from the push dispenser beside the sink. The razor was getting dull and it hurt to shave, but it woke up my flesh.

What I really needed, though, was sleep. If somehow I could make an "Out of Order" sign for the door handle outside, I could stretch out on the counter across the sinks and get in an hour. But there were the beginnings of traffic out in the hallway and no escape route. Perhaps I could go up on the roof, though that was probably where the staff went to smoke.

The problem with the world was that there were no places to just lie down. You should be able to sleep anywhere. As long as it didn't inconvenience anybody, why not? As it was, you needed money. So, get some, then, turn your art into cash. Money was more important than art. Or love: that's just the way it was. And all the people who had the money were busy buying up the remaining corners of the earth and charging you to step on it. So they could earn enough to buy themselves a home in a gated village with walls built to keep everybody out.

Once I started thinking how I could arrange the world better it usually meant I really did need sleep, though now I didn't feel it. When you are awake too long, you don't just get gradually more tired, drowsiness arrives in waves. You feel awake for eight hours, then sleepy for eight, awake for seven, then sleepy for seven, and so on until the frequency is so close together you are simply unconscious. I was moving into a wakeful period now and I judged that it would be another three or four hours at the most before I would crash.

I splashed cold water on my face. What looked back at me from the mirror was an improvement, but something was still not right in my eyes, something furtive, like a dog caught in the garbage. I checked my wallet. Three five-euro bills and some change. I carefully folded one five-euro note into my top breast pocket, checked myself in the mirror one last time, put on my show face and strode out to the front desk. The man behind the desk was talking under his breath to another man, and they both glanced at me then looked away, too quickly. I approached the counter without breaking stride, taking the five-euro note out of my top pocket, and rested my hands on the edge of the counter holding the money in my knuckles. He saw it and changed what he was about to say to: "Yes, sir?"

I asked if I could call up to Aurélie's room. He said certainly, and placed the house phone in front of me on the counter, then turned away politely. I dialled Aurélie's room and let it ring nine times, hung up, turned around, and as though I had summoned her, there she was.

"Oh, hello!" I said.

"Hi!"

I said thank you to the man behind the counter and left the five-euro note. He almost clicked his heels and bowed. I turned back to Aurélie. "Coffee?"

"Why not?"

In the bar off the lobby we found a table set for breakfast. We ordered coffee and asked for a menu. I hoped she would pay for it.

"So what's on for today?" I said. I thought I'd avoid the topic of my manuscript until she brought it up. She seemed almost carefree, like she hadn't read it at all, but that couldn't be. Surely she had been at least curious.

"Well," she said, "there's a talk on 'The Role of Co-incidence in Storytelling' and then there are a few meetings. Also (this is exciting!) I heard in the elevator that Beauchamp and Sillery are about to square off."

"Really? What about?"

"Doesn't matter. They've been at it for years." She actually liked this stuff, and I suppose I could live with that.

But I was confused about Aurélie not mentioning my manuscript. I made my face light up like I had just thought of something. "So, what did you think?" I asked.

"About what?"

"About my journal."

"Sorry. What?"

"I left you ... Oh! Have you checked your mail today?"

"Mail?"

"At the front desk?"

"Yes. Why?"

"Oh."

"What is it?" she asked.

"I left something for you."

"A gift?"

"Yes."

"How nice. So where is it?"

"I should check," I said. "One second." I got up and went out and across to the front desk. The man to whom I had given the five euros asked if he could help me.

"I left an envelope here last night."

"Yes?"

"And I was wondering if it reached the party to whom it was addressed."

"What room would that be, sir?"

I told him the room number that the other clerk had given me the night before. He turned and scanned cubbyholes behind him. "The mail for that room has been picked up, sir."

"I was just talking to the person it was addressed to and she hasn't received it."

"The cubby hole is empty, sir."

"So ..."

"Somebody else might have picked it up for her?"

"No. She's alone."

He looked at the computer screen. "Room 354 is a double room, sir. Perhaps it was picked up by whomever she is sharing the room with?"

I stopped and he waited professionally, trying not to look like a man sympathizing with a jilted lover. Well, I might as well give him that story, if that's what he cared to believe. This could all go toward explaining my suspicious behaviour two days ago. "Ah," I said, like the implications were settling on me. I think I managed to convey to him that the spiritual weight was enormous.

"Are you alright, sir?" he said quietly.

"Yes," I said and walked abstractly away, then once around a corner I snapped out of it. I reckoned that I knew what happened now. I sat down with Aurélie.

"So?" she asked.

"It's been taken."

"Marcel," she said. "Who else? He signed for the room at the beginning of the week and they must have given your gift to him when he came for his key."

"I see," I said.

"Was it expensive?"

"No. Not at all. Just something I've written."

"OK. But the thing is, I don't really want to talk to Marcel about it."

"That's OK," I said. "I will."

"Really?"

"Yes."

"OK. But it's later than I thought now and I'm afraid I'll have to skip breakfast. I have to go listen to some boring talk about The Man Who Liked Horses." She started to gather her things.

"Anything like the one I told you?"

"The Donkey Trader? No. This one's North American. Ojib-Cree. A man likes horses so much that he offends the tribe with his greed. His punishment is that every time he falls asleep he hears the thunder of hooves and has to get up and chase them."

"Not bad."

"Yes. But I'm late." She stood up. "It's supposed to be an hour and a half. I might be able to sneak out early."

"I'll be here."

She left. I paid for the ridiculously overpriced coffee, and after I received the change I counted up my remaining cash and saw that I had less than five euros in my wallet. I stood up and walked out without leaving a tip, but as I left I saw out of the corner of my eye the waiter arrive and register this. I would have to set that right. I crossed the lobby and sat down in a deep chair and waited. Academics were starting to get off the elevator, joining or breaking away from small groups, reintroducing themselves from other conferences. There was an older lady dressed in the severest fashion the academic world allowed. There was a younger man who looked happy and brilliant and full of energy, and at whom the older lady was purposely not smiling. She had seen it all before, and had in fact once been in love with somebody like him. There were two bickering colleagues locked together like binary stars, taking turns acting sceptical at what the other was declaiming.

And there was a man who looked like a spy, standing beside a thin woman with an almost identical face. She looked around for a cigarette, and he stood straight and scanned the room, putting everything in his place, deciding what to use, what not. If I was putting him into a story I would make him a man obsessed by power, dedicating his whole life to either maintaining himself in his position or advancing. Everyone in the room was concerned with this to a degree, me included, but only he was possessed by it every waking moment, and when he slept, he dreamt of it as well. The Man Who Dreamt of Horses, in fact, but how had he offended his tribe?

As a young man he had discovered something about lies, that if you told them, you had the advantage of people who did not: you always knew where they stood, but they never knew that about you.

Yes, but he was also starting to realize what this meant, and how it made the world more meaningless. The fear was starting in his eyes, and the only thing that stopped it from taking over entirely was his obsessive dedication to taking the next step in his advancement, though less and less committed each day, increasingly becoming aware that although he would win, the prize would be worthless ...

The elevator door opened, Marcel came out, and I took a deep breath and stood up. Back into the fray.

"Good morning," I said.

"Oh. Hi."

"You may have picked up a package I left at the front desk."

"What?"

"A brown envelope with some papers inside?" I said.

"I'm sorry. I don't understand."

He looked at me exactly like he didn't know what I was talking about. He was better than I thought. "My mistake," I said.

"No problem," he said, with complete instant forgiveness, flawlessly performed. "Now. About this goat story.

I checked with our database, and there has been no recorded version of it as far as I can tell. There is The Goat of Aleppo, Djoha and the Goat, The Billy-Goat Who Saved the City, and any number of stories about goats butting the visiting parson, but nothing about the Goat in the Tree."

"I see," I said. He was playing me, of course, but his excitement about the story was sincere.

"That means it's bigger than I thought. I don't think it's ever been heard before." He fumbled for a cigarette, put it in his mouth, but didn't light it. "So what we have here," he said, "is a completely untouched story (or cycle of stories for all I know) which could ... possibly add another clue to the workings of a different culture." What he meant was that it could make his reputation in the field. "I mean," he said, "it's post-industrial, for one thing. There is a bus, for instance. That's not unheard of, but the forms and the magic are decidedly ancient, you know?"

I said that I did. I was almost sorry I was setting him up. But I mustn't forget that he was playing me as well.

"Then there is the moral," he said. "I mean, is the storyteller saying that you should behave like the goatherd, or not? It's not a fable or a parable, so what is it?"

What it is, I thought to myself, is a story. And I guess I've known forever that as such it is always more valuable than how it can be categorized. But he was an academic. A story didn't have the same value to him as it had to listeners who came to it with innocent ears, willing to take from it what they could. It was a new plant for a botanist to classify and dissect. Well, it's what they do, the idiots, I thought, with the type of contempt which creeps in when you go into battle, and probably has to creep in, if you are going to win. And if you are not going into battle to win, why go into battle at all?

He held in his hand the pages of the paper I had dictated to him last night and which he had apparently transcribed, and he was now reading over them, cramming for his appearance.

"You'll do fine," I said.

"You think?"

"Sure. Is Hélène coming?"

"I don't know," he said. "I haven't seen her since last night." He frowned quickly, but didn't let himself think about it. "OK." He glanced at his watch. "Time to go. Are you coming?"

"I was hoping to."

He consulted a brochure in his agenda, oriented himself, and led the way down the hall and into a conference room. I followed, and stopped inside the door as he went to set up.

On a dais on the far side of the room there was the speaker's table with three microphones on stands, and in the centre a desktop podium. A banner on the wall behind declared that this was in fact The International Storytelling Conference. The room had no windows, and was lit in a neutral, tiring way, with no shadows or definition, and the silence was muffled and irritating. It was as unlike the Djemma el Fna as it was possible for a place to be. There were maybe a dozen people standing around or sitting, waiting. A man and a woman were at the other door talking in low tones. The young enthusiastic academic came in, walked to the front, looked around and stood scanning the room for someone, then strode out again to get more coffee. A fatigued man sat sprawled on a chair in the back corner, his hands hanging down, waiting. The room itself could have heaved an impatient sigh.

Anthropologists and folklorists began to arrive. People who had lived amongst primitive tribes in far-flung jungles had difficulty getting the doors open. Scholars who had formed alliances with custodians of song-cycles yawned and sat themselves in places which were close enough to the exit so that it would not disrupt anything if they snuck out halfway. The anthropology of anthropologists.

Take a story and put it on tape to eliminate the presence of the storyteller; then, because that voice still expressed something of the original spirit, transcribe its words onto paper. But when you read even that, there are still rhythms that form in your head, and unexpected turns in the narrative. So write a commentary on it to explain the effects and how they are achieved, and to give away in advance how the story will reveal itself, thereby insulating yourself against any wonder whatsoever. What was once a performance is now an autopsy. Next, get a conference together of people who do this for a living and put them in a room with no shadows, together with their rivals who, if they did find themselves caught off-guard for a second and tempted to react innocently, would stifle their reaction lest they would be seen lapsing from objectivity. The worst audience in the world, paid to be judgmental.

I found myself questioning whether we could understand *anything* without wonder ... Well, I hadn't had much sleep last night. My eyes were dry, no matter how much I blinked, and coffee wouldn't help, just make me more nervous. A glass of orange juice would be a lifesaver, but there wasn't any left on the side-table.

Marcel had set up at one end of the head table and was reading over his paper and The Man Who Looked Like A Spy entered with his girl. They moved to the front together and, as she took a seat near the stage, he went to the opposite end of the table from Marcel and sat down, immediately opening his case and going through his papers, not because he had anything to look at, I think, but to give people in the room the opportunity to look at him without embarrassment.

Aurélie came in, saw me, waved a quick wave, and strode over as my spirit lifted. "It was a bore, and I snuck out," she said. "What are you doing here?"

"Come to see the fun."

"You must be desperate," she said.

I was proud to be with her. I was even standing straighter. She looked around, saw Spy-man at his papers with his girl looking on, and turned back to me. Then, strangely, she gave me a quick look-over and straightened my collar. If I'd had my wits about me I would have understood what that meant, but instead the attention from her only made me feel excellent, and I smiled back dopily.

I saw Marcel catch the eye of Spy-man and then flash back a quick lacklustre smile: shake hands and come out fighting. An older man entered, walked to the head table and took the seat behind the table-top podium, checked his watch, looked around for a gavel, found nothing, and so stood up and said loudly: "Right!"

Aurélie and I sat down and the crowd directed its attention towards him. "We're here to listen to Professor Beauchamp who has a paper to read, and then Professor Sillery" — he gestured to Spy-man — "will have a chance to rebut. So, any time you're ready, Professor Beauchamp."

Nobody applauded, and there was an awkward moment as Marcel coughed into his hand and shifted in his chair, which squeaked loudly. "Thank you," he said, and he started to read, but he hadn't finished his first sentence when somebody in the back yelled "Louder!" and he leant into the microphone and rolled on.

Two thirds of the way through the talk he mixed up the pages and had to do a lot of reshuffling to get back on track. His classes at University couldn't have been very popular.

Eventually he got through the argument I had drafted for him the night before. When he finished, I didn't feel in any way triumphant, but I told myself it was for Aurélie, an unselfish act. Why does it have to make *me* feel good, anyhow, I thought, although in my experience an unselfish act usually does.

"That should help you out," I said to Aurélie.

"Why?"

"It's not a traditional folk story."

"What do you mean?"

"I thought it up."

"I don't understand."

"Well, yesterday ..."

But she interrupted: "Shh." And then added something which I was sure she didn't mean but which caught me completely off-guard. "Marcel is going to speak now," she said, and Spy-man, the man who had been introduced as Professor Sillery, stood up and tapped the microphone.

I felt my heart beat suddenly faster, but it was still just possible that Aurélie had misspoken.

The Adjudicator stood up. "All right," he said. "Thank you Marcel Beauchamp. Marcel Sillery will now respond."

Even now there was still a chance that everything was all right, but when I turned to Aurélie to ask her about it, I saw her glance at the back of the girl who was with Marcel Sillery and then almost immediately glance away, suppressing what looked like a sudden stab of hatred. Then I saw her look back toward Marcel Sillery with an expression of carefully contained emotion, and I didn't have to ask myself anything more.

I knew I had failed miserably, and for the stupidest of reasons, because of a type of misunderstanding and coincidence that I would have rejected as unworthy in one of my own stories. I closed my eyes and groaned softly.

"Thank you," said Marcel Sillery. "And I would like to discuss what went on here just now ..." He started like he was sorting things out in his mind. "If I understand what you are saying," he said to the other Marcel, "your case is based on that one story about the goat in the tree?"

"Yes," Marcel answered confidently.

Sillery still acted confused. "But ... you say that you collected it on the Essaouira bus?"

"Yes."

"Yes," said Sillery, not like he was surprised, but to clear up a point for everybody in the room which he needed to establish before he advanced his argument. "Well, *I* contend that there is some question as to whether it *is* in fact a story from *any* oral tradition." He waited, his eyebrows raised.

"I'm sorry," said Marcel. "What do you mean?"

"I have evidence to support the idea that it is a created story," he said, and he drew from beneath some papers in front of him a brown envelope which looked, I thought with a shock, exactly like the one I'd left for Aurélie last night.

But why *should* I be shocked? Of course that's where it would have ended up.

"What evidence?" said Marcel. He was beginning to lose ground while trying to keep up a brave face. I knew how he felt.

"This manuscript, which was left in my letterbox last night, appears to be a journal of some sort and in it the person who wrote it describes how he created the goat story himself."

"But ... what?" said Marcel.

"It's all here," said Marcel Sillery. "So, the question I have is this: is it in a tradition or not? Off-hand I cannot think of another folktale it may be derived from."

Marcel jumped on this. "Well that's the point. It's a totally undiscovered example of a new classification!" But he didn't quite pull it off. You could almost hear the implied question at the end: "Isn't it?" Then he tried to regain some ground by falling back on a sentence which had been handy to him in the past. "I cross-referenced the plot points and I haven't come across anything like it."

"But the document which *I* uncovered seems to describe its recent creation, and if that proves true, then the story is therefore not from *any* folkloric tradition."

"Well I wouldn't know anything about that," Marcel finished lamely.

The adjudicator looked at his watch and stood up. "Thank you, both Marcels: Sillery and Beauchamp ... Um ... I think we can all agree that there have been some interesting developments this morning, and obviously we'll probably need some time to process all of them. I suggest we take a break now, and since this room is booked until two pm, we can reconvene back here then."

Marcel Sillery gathered his papers, pushed back his chair, stood up, stepped off the riser and without looking at my Marcel, Orange Marcel, he went to his girl and together they both strode out of the room.

Questioning babble broke out, and people rose to their feet. My Marcel's eyes, under confused and defeated brows, followed him. His shoulders were slumped forward and his lower lip was heavy. He blinked twice and slowly raised his head to look around. His eyes found me and stayed. I had betrayed him.

I looked away. We stood up and I started to move Aurélie toward the exit, avoiding looking back at Marcel.

"What's Marcel up to?" said Aurélie in a whisper to me.

"He's found a new story, and he thought he'd be able to get funding for it."

"No. Not Marcel *Beauchamp*. He's an idiot. I'm talking about Marcel *Sillery*. You know. The Marcel I was talking to you about last night." Which all confirmed what I already knew. The dull bolt inside me turned once more. I groaned again.

Aurélie looked right at me. "What did you do?" she said.

"I set up Marcel. Marcel who read the paper. Marcel Beauchamp."

"What do you mean 'set him up'?"

"I told him this story about a goat ... He liked it. I said I heard it from an old source, but I made it up."

"That's 'The Goat in the Tree'?"

"Yes. I thought it would help you."

"How was telling Marcel Beauchamp a story and saying ... I don't understand."

"I thought Marcel Beauchamp was *your* Marcel."

"My Marcel? Marcel *Beauchamp*?" She looked at me like she was going to spit. "You thought I was going with Marcel *Beauchamp*. I mean, *look* at him for godsakes. He's ... *orange*."

"How am I supposed to know what sort of men you like?" I said. I was nettled. I had only been trying to help.

She seemed to realize that this wasn't getting anywhere and brought things back to the matter at hand. "Ok ... So. You told him a story and he thought it was a folktale."

"Yes. Because I thought it would help you out, but it didn't ... OK. That's not important now ... Look. I just figured you could do what Marcel, *your* Marcel, just did to my Marcel, Orange Marcel."

"Did what?"

"Knock him down a few notches. Get back on top. Have something on him." When I heard myself say it, it sounded incredibly unworthy and stupid.

"Well I still don't understand ..." But she understood something, because she sounded disappointed. Oh God. This was going to be worse than I thought.

The Muse who watches over you is a benevolent Muse, and from her flows all things that grow. I looked around for her but she was nowhere to be seen. Just other people trying to find their Muses too. I wondered whether they didn't all sometimes dream that what they'd really like is just to make something, some product or poem or prophecy, which they drop into the world and which simply spreads by its own usefulness or beauty, and is passed along freely from one person to another until it's everywhere on its own, making the world that much better for it being there. I also wondered whether, having given up any hope of ever finding that, they had decided instead to kill time with manipulation and politics. And I had willingly stepped into that world.

"And what was all that about a manuscript?" said Aurélie.

"It was my journal. I wrote it for you. Last night I left it in your mail at the reception desk but it ended up in the wrong hands. I wrote it because I thought I should be honest with you."

"You mean *start* being honest?" she said, though I didn't know what she could have meant by that, knowing what she did about me, so I put it down to her anger. A step behind her, I followed her down a hall and turned a corner past some people from the conference. She cooled down and turned toward me. "It was Marcel's room too," she said. "So that explains how he got it."

"Yes."

"And now he has something on Marcel Beauchamp."

"He also has my journal."

"Well, what's in it?"

So I told her. Trying to get the facts straight, I didn't tell it right, but stumbled all over the place. She found it difficult to follow and kept asking questions which threw me off the track further. Parts of it I didn't tell at all, just the bare-bones. I couldn't snap myself out of it. Would I ever find your favour again, O Muse?

Aurélie listened to it all, then we walked out into the gardens behind the hotel. She didn't say anything as we followed a foot-path lined with old olive trees with braided trunks and orange trees pruned into spheres. I was inside the garden now, but I didn't know what I could do about anything. Hotel employees looked at me like they were wondering whether they should ask if I was bothering her. We came to the far wall and she sat on a park bench. I sat beside her.

"We can still handle this," she said suddenly. I wondered if she meant us together. "He's got your journal, so he knows the goat story's a fake."

"Yes."

"Well, what about if we said your journal was a fake."

"I don't follow."

"Fiction. Say you really *did* hear the goat story, and were writing it into a *novel*. That's it! Say that the manuscript Marcel Sillery read is the draft of a novel you're writing."

It was everything I shouldn't have done, but I was over the edge now. At least I could be with her while she hatched her plan.

"There's something else," I said.

"What?"

"The widow. Remember the storyteller where I first met you? In The Djemma?"

"Yes."

"Well, it's kind of complicated ..."

"Go ahead."

"This was all in my journal, but ... you see ... I don't speak Arabic."

"Really?" she said, almost sarcastically.

"No. I made up that story."

"Don't worry. I already figured that out," she said.

I looked at her. "But ..."

"I *do* speak Arabic," she said.

I paused. "Really?" It was the only thing I could think of saying.

"My Grandmother was from Algeria."

"So ... you knew."

"Yes."

"So ... Why?"

"I was interested in you," she said. "You tell a good story, and I wondered what your game was." And then she added: "Also ... I was *interested* in you." Past tense.

"Oh."

"Yes."

Then I remembered what I had started to say. "Anyhow. That widow, she really *is* telling the goat story now. In the Djemma."

"What?"

"The widow is telling the Goat In the Tree." And I told her how I had spent that night at Nuradeen's.

"OK," she said. "That's good to know. In fact, it's perfect."

"Yes."

She stood up. "We'll have to let Marcel Sillery build his argument, let him think he's on top. This is good." She was getting quite excited about it. "Let him walk way out on a limb with it ..." She paused, then decided. "OK. I'll organize a meeting with Gilles Doiron. You can tell him that it was the draft of a novel." I didn't know who Gilles Doiron was, but it was in her hands now. I would to whatever she said, but I never felt less excitement for anything. She looked at me. "You will have to be able to do it convincingly."

"Yes. OK," I said. "I was just thinking ..."

"What?"

"Nothing."

"I'll line up a meeting, then." And she left.

I continued to sit. The sun beat down and wherever the garden was lit it was so bright you had to squint when you looked at it. On the other side of the wall an electric wire sagged between two poles and a lone turtle dove balanced at its low point. I was thirsty. There was a bar on the patio by the hotel where they undoubtedly charged more for a drink than I now possessed, but apart from that I don't know whether I could get away with even sitting there without Aurélie by my side to lend some credibility to my presence. I did in fact have a professional reason to be here now and if anybody asked I could say that I had a meeting with someone at the storytelling conference. But I looked like a bum. And I felt worse, bone weary, right at the bottom of the low end of the cycle of fatigue.

Part of it was what I had done to Orange Marcel. I didn't know I would do him harm, or rather I knew I would, but thought he deserved it, so it was a mistake, but I had nevertheless hurt an almost complete stranger. There was a responsibility there ... And now everything was effort.

HERE'S NOT MUCH more to tell. I waited until she came back: Aurélie, my love no longer. She was with Gilles Doiron, the head of her department, who turned out to be the adjudicator from the conference room. He asked me if what Aurélie had told him was true, and I said yes. Was I a novelist? he asked, and I lied: Not a published one yet unfortunately, but hopeful. He nodded his head. "We'll need some more proof about the story," he said.

"Go see the widow in the Djemma," I said. "Aurélie can show you where she works."

She gave me a quick secret glance of approval, but it was only professional. "Can you speak Arabic?" I asked Doiron.

"Not a word, unfortunately," he said.

"Well, Aurélie can translate for you," I said.

And Aurélie confirmed that she would. We would have made a good team.

"OK. We'll do that," he said, and then: "Good luck with your novel." He rose, shook hands with me and left.

"Next is Marcel Beauchamp," Aurélie said.

We walked back to the patio bar where he was sitting. I was more sleepy than I'd ever been in my life.

Marcel looked up. "What did I ever do to you?" he said.

"I'm sorry," I said. "It's all been a huge misunderstanding."

"It's alright, though," Aurélie said. "The story *was* a folktale."

"What are you talking about?" He looked at me. "I thought you wrote in that journal that you thought up the story yourself."

"No," I said. "*He* said that: Marcel Sillery. But he was reading from my novel. He just *thought* it was a journal." Marcel stared blankly so I started again. "The Journal. The one Sillery has. It's a *novel* ..." We went through the explanation that Aurélie and I had agreed on. It took a while to make him understand. He had started his drinking for the day.

"Wait," he said when he was almost convinced. "Why did you look so guilty then?"

"When?"

"In the conference room. After he embarrassed me."

"Because it was supposed to be for Aurélie to read, not Marcel," I said.

"That's true," said Aurélie, seeing where I was going.

"The point is," I said, "everything I've told you has been the truth." Which itself was a lie. Not a story, a *lie*. And if you want to know what I found out then, it is this: The difference between a storyteller and a liar is that at the centre of the liar is an empty place.

He didn't follow all the steps in the argument, but he saw that the power was shifting back and away from Marcel Sillery, and he was willing to be pushed along with it.

"Anyhow," said Aurélie, "you two had better start getting used to each other."

"Why?" said Marcel.

"Because Doiron *liked* your speech, Marcel. The role of the audience in a story is a subject he's been meaning to address for a while." Which was news to me.

"Oh?" said Marcel with a little light of hope starting in his eyes.

"Yes."

"Hunh!" he said with a note of pride for his work, misplaced, I thought, since he hadn't, after all, even written the damned thing. Having his boss think he did the work was as important to him as actually doing the work itself. Hence the fear. "I have another paper coming up in a month," he said. "I'll need some more examples ..."

And I owed him that at least. "How about The Guitar Player and His Girl?"

"Remind me what happened there?"

"She dies, and he goes to Hell to rescue her."

"Oh? How?"

"By singing songs ..."

I spoke with the Orange Man as he drank and took notes. After I redeemed myself with him, I might be able to get some more money out of their department, but if not, then I suppose I could go back to the Djemma and see what opportunities presented themselves. If there was nothing there for me I would go to the Embassy and be sent back to France, or perhaps try to make my way to Senegal, or New Caledonia or Martinique, though by what means I didn't know yet. What I did know was that my very freedom now seemed only to weigh me down. I needed sleep. Everything would be better if I could just get some sleep.

ABOUT THE AUTHOR

Lorne Elliott is perhaps best known as the host for ten years of CBC Radio's *Madly Off In All Directions* and is a musician, comedian, playwright and novelist. He has written and performed in numerous plays and shows in various media. His latest musical play, *Jamie Rowsell Lives*, won the 2012 Playwrights Guild of Canada Award for Best Musical. He has had a novella, *The Fixer-Upper* and a novel, *Beach Reading*, previously published. Visit his website at www.lorne-elliott.com.

PRAISE FOR HIS PREVIOUS WORK

Bill Richardson, writer and broadcaster:

With his first novel, that mad genius Lorne Elliott offers a coming of age story that's both antic and lyrical. There are the snappy riffs and measured mayhem and bouts of lunacy you'd expect from so seasoned a stand-up comedian. But pages are also graced and enlivened by lore and by learning; by a real passion for nature, history and music; by an ear attuned to the bittersweet singing of the human heart. Good for the beach, good for the fireside, good for under the covers, good for Lorne: *Beach Reading* is a treat, stem to stern.

Terry Fallis, author of
The Best Laid Plans *and* Up and Down:

In *Beach Reading*, Lorne Elliott masterfully creates a wacky and wonderful world beyond the red sand of Price Edward Island's travel ads. By turns, hilarious and melancholy, but mostly hilarious, Elliott's sure hands will keep the pages turning as his memorable rogues and rebels worm their way right into your heart. This is storytelling at its finest.

Patrick Ledwell, writer and comedian:

Elliott is this country's Mark Twain. *Beach Reading* is schooled in the same storytelling tradition, where a young narrator strings together beautiful incongruities, in a wandering way. But what begins as picaresque ambling soon coalesces into an artful path, and the open-throated laughter makes a straight route to your heart.

RECYCLED
Paper made from
recycled material
FSC® C100212
FSC
www.fsc.org

Printed in December 2013
by Gauvin Press,
Gatineau, Québec